BBC
DOCTOR WHO

BBC CHILDREN'S BOOKS

UK | USA | Canada | Ireland | Australia
India | New Zealand | South Africa

BBC Children's Books are published by Puffin Books,
part of the Penguin Random House group of companies
whose addresses can be found at global.penguinrandomhouse.com.

www.penguin.co.uk
www.puffin.co.uk
www.ladybird.co.uk

Penguin
Random House
UK

First published 2016
001

Written by Trevor Baxendale
Copyright © BBC Worldwide Limited, 2016

Printed in Great Britain by Clays Ltd, St Ives plc

A CIP catalogue record for this book is available from the British Library

ISBN: 978–1–405–92651–5

All correspondence to:
BBC Children's Books
Penguin Random House Children's
80 Strand, London WC2R 0RL

BBC

DOCTOR WHO

CHOOSE THE FUTURE

TERROR MOON

TREVOR BAXENDALE

PUFFIN

HOW TO USE THIS BOOK

With this *Choose the Future* book, YOU are in control of the Doctor's story from the very first page to the very last. Every decision you make affects his future – the fate of the universe he protects is in your hands!

Read the first entry, choose what the Doctor should do next, then turn to the number of the entry of your choice. The adventure will unfold as you make new decisions and pick new numbers all the way through the story.

If you think you're ready to embark on a dangerous escapade alongside the Doctor – likely to involve the odd alien nemesis, several perilous encounters, plus an awful lot of running – then turn the page to begin . . .

1

Far out in deep space, beyond the Silver Devastation, an orphan moon drifts through the endless night.

Clinging to the rocky surface of the moon is a series of life-support modules connected by airlocks and transit tubes. This was once a small human outpost, but it now appears abandoned. The base portholes are all dark. A spaceship stands unused on a launch pad. A deathly quiet seeps through the shadowy interior of the outpost, and the air is thick and cold.

Inside one of the modules, the silence is abruptly broken by a loud, raucous wheezing. An old blue police box materialises out of nowhere, landing with a solid thump in the middle of a darkened room. The door bangs suddenly open and a tall, gaunt figure wearing a frock coat over a hoodie leaps out. It is the Doctor, that mysterious wanderer through time and space, and he is not happy.

He is, in fact, furious.

The cause of his bad temper is the police box – his TARDIS – which is malfunctioning yet again.

It seems to have a mind of its own these days, the Doctor thinks sourly. The time machine never takes him where he wants to go: he'd been aiming for the Eye of Orion, a galactic beauty spot famed for its relaxing negative ions, but somehow he'd ended up here . . . wherever here is.

The Doctor's boots scrape loudly on a hard floor and the noise echoes around metallic walls. He can't really see anything. It's too dark to be sure, but it feels like a laboratory of some kind. He is about to ask his companion to fetch a torch from the TARDIS when he remembers that he is, for once, travelling alone. Another reason why he is feeling so bad-tempered. He likes company. He doesn't much like this cold, ominous place.

The Doctor stands and scowls into the darkness for a minute, debating his next course of action.

If you think the Doctor should return to the TARDIS, go to 2.

If you think he should stay and explore, go to 3.

2

The Doctor turns back to the TARDIS. The Eye of Orion is so beautiful in this era that it would be a shame not to try again. Perhaps a drop of oil on the helmic regulator would help? The TARDIS couldn't get it wrong twice in a row, surely.

The Doctor takes a last look at the gloomy room. It has all the markings of a laboratory of some kind. The urge to stop and explore is very strong – but it's not much fun without someone to explore with. Plus, the light from inside the TARDIS is warm and welcoming.

But, just before he reaches it, the TARDIS door slowly closes.

The Doctor straightens, his nerves bristling. That shouldn't happen. He reaches out and pushes the door back open. It swings slowly inward with a creak. The hinges clearly need oiling as well, just like the helmic regulator.

The Doctor steps cautiously into his time-and-space machine. This isn't the usual way he walks into his TARDIS. Normally he barges straight in, brimming with enthusiasm for the next trip, or rushing back to the controls in a frantic race against time, or . . .

He stops inside and closes the door behind him. Everything looks normal. The control console is humming, lights flashing across its hexagonal surface. The central column is pulsing with a soft orange light, rising up to meet the huge, concentric time rotors above.

Yes, everything looks normal, the Doctor reflects. But what if someone – or something – crept into the TARDIS while his back was turned? The Doctor's brow furrows with annoyance as he remembers bursting out of the TARDIS and leaving the door wide open behind him.

The Doctor crosses quietly to the console, allowing his long fingers to trail across the buttons and levers as he thinks about what to do next. Perhaps he is just imagining things. Perhaps he has been alone for too long. Surely nothing could have entered the TARDIS without his knowledge?

If you think the Doctor should check the TARDIS for an intruder, go to 4.

If you think he should dematerialise the TARDIS, go to 5.

3

'Lights,' says the Doctor.

Voice-activated photonic projectors raise the light level. The Doctor is standing in the middle of an extensive laboratory littered with advanced scientific equipment.

Behind the ducting, something scuttles into the shadows. The Doctor peers under the edge of the ducting, but he can't see anything unusual.

Apart from a dead body, that is.

A human being in white overalls is sprawled across the floor, hidden from immediate view by a workbench. The Doctor has seen many corpses – both human and alien, in countless times and places – but seldom anything as strange as this.

At first the Doctor thinks the poor man has been skinned alive; the face is just a contortion of exposed muscle and bone. But, as the Doctor watches, the raw sinew disappears, stripped away to reveal the naked skull beneath. The overalls sag, relieved of their shape as the flesh disintegrates, and settle on skeletal remains.

The Doctor's eyes grow dark and angry. This is not the work of anything natural.

If you think the Doctor should examine the body further, go to 19.

If you think he should take another look for the thing in the ducting, go to 21.

4

The Doctor glances quickly around the console room. His eyes narrow. His brows bristle. He can't shake the feeling that there is something in here with him. Something alien.

But then, he is an alien too. Everyone is. It's all a matter of perspective.

The Doctor circles the control console, his gaze darting around the room. Something on the walkway that circles the chamber holds his attention. Was it a movement? Something creeping into the shadow of a bookcase?

The Doctor bounds up the steps that lead to the walkway. There are many bookcases standing innocently against the TARDIS walls. Nothing could get behind them. In fact, very little could hide up here. Apart from books.

'Hello?' he says eventually. 'Is there anybody or anything in here? Besides me, I mean. And the books, of course.'

Silence is the only reply.

The Doctor snatches one of the books at random from a shelf. '*The Invisible Man*, by H. G. Wells,' he reads aloud. 'Hmm.'

There is a soft noise from downstairs and the Doctor turns sharply. He feels the hairs rise on the back of his neck: he's been looking in the wrong place.

Go to 6.

5

The Doctor pushes the dematerialisation lever forward with abrupt purpose.

The time rotors begin to turn, the engines grind, the glass column at the centre of the console glows with an intense orange light. With a loud wheezing and groaning noise, the TARDIS leaves the moonbase and transfers itself into the mysterious time–space Vortex.

The Doctor's long fingers flicker over the controls, setting coordinates, adjusting for all the various factors that affect the passage of his time machine through the Vortex, not least of which is the ship's great age.

'Come on,' he urges the TARDIS. 'The Eye of Orion! Negative ions and wonderful ice cream!' He twists the helmic regulator with a flourish and the great cogs counter-rotate above his head. 'No more gloomy space stations!'

The TARDIS flits through light years and across the

centuries . . . and, just as the Doctor begins to relax and smile, something climbs on to his back and digs sharp pincers deep into his neck.

There *was* something else aboard the TARDIS!

The talons bite deep, and the Doctor feels something invading his mind. He tries to fight it but the thing has him in an iron grip!

If you think the Doctor should pull the lever again and materialise the TARDIS, go to 8.

If you think he should use the telepathic circuits instead, go to 49.

6

The Doctor walks slowly down to the console level. His boots echo on the steps. He feels nervous, something he is not accustomed to in his own TARDIS. He doesn't like it. It makes him feel cross.

There's only one place an intruder could be hiding now: below the console, down where the TARDIS power core and control circuits are located.

As he heads towards the stairs that lead down from the console level, the Doctor pauses. On the edge of the console is a pair of stylish sunglasses. These are the Doctor's sonic sunglasses, highly advanced wearable tech that he developed, almost on a whim, to replace his old, broken sonic screwdriver. They are incredibly useful and rather cool.

But then so was his electric guitar, propped up on its stand by the Magpie Electricals amplifier. The Doctor played the guitar to help himself think, or so he liked people to believe.

Actually, he just liked playing it. It was a loud and beautiful instrument. Very loud!

If you think the Doctor should pick up his sonic sunglasses, go to 9.
If you think he should play his electric guitar instead, go to 22.

7

This time the Doctor emerges from the TARDIS more cautiously, picking up his sonic sunglasses on the way.

Pausing on the threshold between dimensions, he allows his eyes to adjust to the dark. The sunglasses' night-vision setting would help, but he doesn't need them just yet. The light from the TARDIS interior is enough, stretching his shadow out ahead of him.

The laboratory is silent – save for an incongruous ticking from somewhere in the shadows. On a workbench in the corner of the room, a test-tube rolls gently back and forth. Something must have passed it by; something moving quickly and furtively enough to set it rocking. The glass clinks quietly, like a crystal clock ticking away brittle seconds.

The Doctor stops the clock by placing one long finger on the glass. He listens intently to the silence that remains.

It is the silence of a crypt, he thinks. *Thick with death.*

His gaze follows the route he imagines an un-imaginary being might take and settles on the plastic ducting that runs along the lower edge of one of the lab walls.

There are open vents with dark spaces inside.

The perfect hiding place for the creature from the TARDIS.

Go to 21.

8

The Doctor's fingers play quickly across the controls and the giant cogs above the console grind into motion. The central column fills with an amber brilliance, the ancient machinery groans and wheezes, and the TARDIS slowly dematerialises.

The Doctor isn't sure if he has set the correct coordinates – or even, really, what they are. He seems to be working in a trance. The time spent in the Vortex is relative and unknowable; the Doctor barely registers it.

Eventually the time rotor slows to a halt and the TARDIS lands. The hum of its powerful instruments fills the room. The destination monitor flickers into life:

EARTH. HUMANIAN ERA. CENTURY 21.

As if in a dream, the Doctor heads for the exit.

Outside it's an overcast day, with the threat of rain heavy in the air. The Doctor inhales deeply, closes his eyes. It's not quite home, but . . .

There's someone walking towards him. A woman. The Doctor frowns, trying to focus. She's wearing a raincoat and a scarf. Blonde hair, serious expression.

Does he know that face?

Go to 14.

9

The Doctor picks up the sunglasses and slips them into the breast pocket of his velvet jacket. After all, whatever is waiting for him below decks might not be a music lover.

Taking a deep breath, the Doctor makes his way down the stairs to the power core. He looks around the chamber, eyes large as saucers beneath bristling brows, not knowing what to expect. He isn't used to intruders in his TARDIS.

'Come out, come out, wherever you are,' he murmurs.

He can't see anything untoward, apart from the cables and calibration equipment left over from a previous attempt to fix the temporal dilation circuit.

He puts on his sonic sunglasses and scans the shadowy area behind the glowing artron cache that lies beneath the control console. Something is hiding behind the tangle of pulsating cables.

The deep hum of the TARDIS power core reverberates

around the room, vibrating through the soles of the Doctor's boots as he creeps slowly across the floor. He can see a distinct shape forming in the shadows – something that might almost be human . . . or might not.

If you think the shape is human, go to 10.

If you think it isn't human, go to 11.

10

The Doctor gently pulls aside the heavy cable and sees a young woman curled up in a foetal position and clearly terrified.

'There are many things to be scared of in this universe,' the Doctor tells her, 'but I am not one of them.'

Her eyes are still full of fear, but behind the fear the Doctor can detect a sharp intelligence. He takes in the white overalls favoured by scientists in the thirty-third century, and scans her name tag: EVA. So, a scientist – presumably with a rational, sensible mind. What could have affected such a person so badly?

'Please,' she says, in barely more than a whisper. 'Please don't send me back out there.'

He regards her coolly for a long moment. She stands up slowly, but she's still trembling, and there is a sheen of perspiration on her skin.

'Well, you used the magic word twice, so that's a good start,' he says. 'Let's do the introductions. You're Eva, and I'm the Doctor –'

Eva's eyes roll up into her head, and she slumps unconscious into the Doctor's arms.

Go to 12.

11

It's something very dark, and very inhuman.

The Doctor can just make out an oily mass atop a forest of spidery legs. A variety of eyes – some the size of marbles, others like tangerines – surround a central, spherical head that looks like a giant black cyst.

'Hello,' the Doctor says, a little more warily than he intends.

The creature chitters back, and the Doctor is reminded, uncomfortably, of the noise a rattlesnake makes just before it strikes.

'I'm the Doctor,' he says, as unthreateningly as he can manage. Sometimes not even that is easy. 'I mean you no harm.'

The dark eyes glisten. A hole opens stickily in the centre of the cyst-head, emitting a gust of foul-smelling breath.

'Well, that's the problem with non-anthropoid types,' the Doctor mutters. 'It's almost impossible to tell what you're thinking just by looking at you. Is that a frown? Because you're looking at the universe's greatest expert in frowning.'

The Doctor attempts a friendly smile, but he knows this can be something of a double-edged sword for him; in the past, his smile has been known to trigger fear, loathing, deep suspicion, and on one memorably unfortunate occasion an interplanetary war.

The creature is unimpressed.

'Yes, I always thought smiling was overrated too,' says the Doctor.

The creature flexes its long legs. Is it preparing to leap? The Doctor eyes it carefully, looking for any sign of increased tension in those curling, multijointed limbs. The eyes remain unreadable.

The Doctor wants to examine the creature more closely, but the thing moves before he can adjust his sonic sunglasses.

It is unbelievably quick; one moment it's cowering behind some cables, and the next it's gone, scuttling behind the

Time Lord and leaping on to his back.

The Doctor whirls, thrashing his arms in an effort to shake off the creature, but it grips hard with its many finger-like legs.

Then he feels the sting. Something has penetrated his neck and shoulders, sending a piercing pain through his skull.

With a sharp, despairing cry he staggers back towards the stairs.

Go to 20.

'Well,' says the Doctor, surprised. 'I know meeting me is a privilege, but there's no need to go weak at the knees.'

Eva takes a shuddering breath as the Doctor helps her up the steps to the console level. He eases her into a chair and examines her quickly.

'You're really not very well,' the Doctor mutters. 'Why is there never a doctor around when you need one?'

'Plague,' says Eva, recovering slightly. Her eyes are hooded. 'The base is under quarantine.'

'What?' The Doctor looks aghast. 'What kind of plague? Is there anyone else on the base? Any other survivors?'

'We're all dead,' she replies. 'Every one of us.'

'You're very much alive. Unwell, but alive.'

'It's only a matter of time . . . it gets everyone in the end.'

'What does? What kind of plague are we talking about?' The Doctor turns to the control console and runs a series of checks. A picture of Eva appears on the monitor screen as the TARDIS scans her.

The Doctor frowns deeply. 'That's very odd. Very odd indeed. In fact, it's quite extraordinary.'

Go to 15.

13

The rat looks up at the Doctor with dark, bead-like eyes.

'Hello, rat,' says the Doctor sadly. He hates it when animals are used for scientific research.

The rat squeaks.

'I'm afraid there's no one left alive,' replies the Doctor. 'You're the only survivor.'

The rat squeaks again.

'Well, there's the rub.' The Doctor sighs heavily. 'There's a good chance you're already infected, like all your mates here.'

The rat squeaks again.

'I don't know,' the Doctor says. 'All the humans are dead. It may not be possible to save you.'

The rat squeaks some more, and the Doctor raises an eyebrow. 'No, I'm not human. Kind of you to notice.'

The rat squeaks and shuffles around its glass cell.

'Well, if you're sure . . .' The Doctor unseals the module

and lets the rat out. It runs up the Doctor's sleeve and sits on his shoulder. It squeaks hurriedly into his ear. 'Pleased to meet you, Scjdd. That's a difficult name for me to pronounce, not being a rodent. Can I call you Skid? I'm the Doctor, by the way. I'm not sure what you're doing here, but I've got a nasty suspicion.'

If you think Skid is infected with malignocites, go to 27.

If you don't think he's infected, go to 39.

14

'Doctor?' The woman walks forward, cautiously at first, a look of concern on her face. Her hands remain deep in the pockets of her raincoat.

'I know you,' the Doctor blurts. 'UNIT person. Brigadier Lethbridge-Stewart's daughter.'

'It's Kate Stewart,' she replies, with an uncertain smile.

The Doctor's knees tremble ominously. Kate starts forward but stops short of helping. She eyes him suspiciously.

The Doctor looks up with his eyes full of both pain and surprise. 'What are you doing here?'

'The space–time telegraph you left Dad,' Kate says. 'It fired up as soon as you were on your way.' Her eyes narrow slightly. 'What's the matter?'

'There's something on my back,' the Doctor gasps. 'Some kind of malignant parasite, hooked into my mind.'

'I can't see anything.'

'It's invisible.'

'So you've brought an invisible alien mind parasite to Earth? How very considerate of you.'

'It's not as if I can control it!'

'Oh, that's even better. Is there any way to get rid of it?'

'Perhaps. But then it might just attack the nearest intelligent life form – which is probably you.'

If you think the Doctor should try to find a way to get rid of the parasite, go to 52.

If you think he should try to keep it away from Kate first, go to 60.

15

'I'm afraid your condition is worse than I thought, Eva,'
explains the Doctor. 'If you were suffering from a disease or
infection, it could be cured.'

'But?'

'Your bloodstream is crawling with nanites – microscopic
machines built using manipulated atoms.'

'Malignocites.'

'An apt name. Not, however, any kind of natural plague.
That would be simple to deal with. Nanotechnology is not.'

'But I'm feeling much better now.'

'That's because you're inside the TARDIS. The nanites –
the malignocites – are held in temporary stasis. Step outside
and they will simply reactivate.'

'And I'll die?'

'Yes.' The Doctor walks round the control console, his eyes
remaining fixed on Eva. 'The question is: what do we do next?'

'I can stay in here, can't I?'

'Can you? Forever? You'll have to step outside some time. I can't eliminate the nanites in here. It's possible that there is equipment that could do it . . . out there.' He points at the exit doors. 'Something happened on this base to infect you with these malignocites. Maybe we can find something to un-infect you.'

If you think Eva should go back outside with the Doctor, go to 16.

If you think Eva should stay safe in the TARDIS, go to 61.

'It'll be risky,' the Doctor says. 'The moment we step out of the TARDIS, those nanites will continue with their work – whatever that is.'

Eva looks downcast. 'They'll kill me. It's what happened to all the others.'

'Yes, but why?' the Doctor wonders, striding towards the outer doors. 'The nanites are technological constructions. Who made them, and what for?'

Eva follows the Doctor out of the TARDIS, shivering. It's cold, but worse than that is the knowledge that the malignocites in her bloodstream have reactivated.

'Lights,' says Eva quietly, and the laboratory is suddenly illuminated.

'Voice-activated photonic projectors,' notes the Doctor approvingly. 'Very swish. At least we can see what we're – oh.'

His voice drops as he sees a pale figure lying on a

workbench. It's a man in white overalls similar to those worn by Eva laid out as if on a mortuary slab.

'This is Michaels,' explains Eva, hugging herself for warmth. 'He was one of the last to be infected.'

As the Doctor examines him, Michaels' eyes suddenly snap open and his hand reaches up to grasp the Doctor's coat.

'Help ussss . . .'

'I thought you were dead!' the Doctor gasps, prising the man's fingers from his lapel. 'I'm very sorry – my mistake.'

Michaels lets out a groan of despair, his eyes wild and bloodshot.

The Doctor glances accusingly at Eva. 'I thought you said there were no survivors!'

'He's near the end,' she replies. 'It won't be long now.'

The Doctor helps Michaels up. The man's breathing is harsh and ragged, heaving in and out in long, agonising gasps.

'I'd look away if I were you,' says Eva.

The Doctor gives her a hard stare and then turns back to Michaels. The man's fingers dig into the Doctor's arms.

'Help ussss . . .'

And then something extraordinary happens. Michaels' skin fades away, leaving only muscle and sinew. Then that also begins to vanish, layer by layer, leaving veins and arteries visible for a brief moment until they too are gone.

The Doctor is left holding nothing more than a skeleton.

Go to 18.

17

The Doctor sinks to the ground as the alien toxins infiltrate his system. He doesn't know how many times he's been stung, but he knows when death is upon him. He has felt it many times before.

He closes his eyes and waits for his Time Lord body to purge itself of the damage, to change, to renew. Soon his entire molecular structure will dissolve in a glowing halo of light, out of which something wondrous and new will appear –

'Doctor! Wake up!'

The voice is loud, urgent, insistent.

'Wake up, Doctor. It's Kate. You're not going to die on me now!'

The Doctor opens his eyes. Kate is looking down at him, her face full of angry concern. 'You look better. Very annoyed, but better.' He reaches a shaking hand towards the mark on her face, where the creature stung her.

'I'm not having a great day, Doctor, and I've used up my meagre supply of patience. Why don't you just tell me what's happening?'

'I'm regenerating,' he tells her.

'Oh no you're not. I'm just getting used to Old Mr Grumpy Doctor. To be perfectly honest, I quite like him. So get up!' Kate digs her hands under the Doctor's arms and pulls him into a sitting position. 'You're coming with me.'

A couple of UNIT squaddies join her and help to carry the Doctor away. The last thing he hears is the sound of gunfire.

Go to 62.

18

The Doctor's face is more drawn than ever. He fixes Eva with a piercing glare.

'We have to find a way to save you, and fast,' he says. He paces quickly around the lab, examining every piece of equipment. 'We need to reverse the nanite programming somehow.'

'Will this do it?' wonders Eva, pointing to a complex piece of machinery shaped like an ancient Egyptian sarcophagus. 'We used it for cellular regulation after exposure to cosmic rays.'

The Doctor's eyes light up. 'Just the thing!' But his eyes suddenly darken as another thought comes to him. 'It will take some time to set this machine up to do exactly what we want. Do we have that time?'

Eva holds up a hand. Her skin is already translucent. 'It's starting, Doctor!'

'If we use the machine now, it could kill you,' the Doctor replies. 'It might not. But it could.'

'And if we wait?'

'It might take too long to set it up correctly and you'll die before we can use it.'

If you think the Doctor should fix the machine properly first, go to 26.

If you think he should risk it and use the machine straight away, go to 30.

19

There's not much left of the body to examine.

The Doctor checks the overalls and finds some basic ID, but it means very little to him. Name, species, planet of origin. Meaningless stuff, except that it might indicate the inhabitants of the base are – or were – all from disparate species and homeworlds.

But this was a human being, the Doctor reminds himself. *Living, thinking, laughing, loving . . . all the things a human being can do.* Now it is nothing more than bones.

He fishes out his sonic screwdriver and scans the remains. There's an invisible residue on the bones: millions of microscopic machines. Nanites.

'They're malignocites,' says a voice from behind him.

He doesn't look up. He had heard the soft tread of the woman as she came into the room. 'And you are?' he asks.

'Jiao,' she replies. 'Research assistant to Professor Hendrick.'

'I'm the Doctor. Malignocites, you say? Good name. Malignant is certainly the word for it. These things have gobbled up your professor like a swarm of very hungry nanomachines, which is exactly what they are.'

If you think the Doctor should warn Jiao to stay back, go to 70.

If you think he should get her to take a closer look, go to 111.

20

In agony, the Doctor crawls back up to the console deck. He can feel the creature's sharp snout working its way deeper into his neck, minute tendrils extending from the tip and burying deep into his spinal column. Like a fast-spreading growth of mould fibres, the malign cells infiltrate his nervous system. The pain is unbearable, but the Doctor is more unsettled by the fact that those fibres are heading for his brain . . . for the centre of his being. His self. His *true* self. And there is nothing he can do to stop it.

He opens his mouth to cry out but all that emerges is a thin string of drool.

Slowly, slowly, the Doctor reaches for the edge of the console and hauls himself to his feet. The controls swim in his vision.

Did I decide to stand up, the Doctor wonders, *or did the creature make me do it?* Is it operating him like a puppet, firing commands through his nervous system instead of pulling strings?

But if the Doctor is aware of what's going on, surely he has a choice? A dark thought crosses his mind, perhaps planted there by the creature: *I could surrender myself, just a little, and find out what it wants . . .*

If you think the Doctor should fight to regain his mind, go to 56.

If you think he should surrender to the creature, go to 8.

21

On his hands and knees, the Doctor peers into the ducting. He can't see a thing; it's too dark. He uses the night-vision function on his sonic sunglasses to look, but can see nothing but dust.

Something black shuffles into the shadows.

'Gotcha,' whispers the Doctor.

The ducting is long and thin, but fortunately so is the Doctor. He threads his arms and shoulders into the vent, and then pushes himself inside using his knees and feet. It's very tight.

'Perhaps this wasn't such a great idea,' he mutters to himself. Cobwebs swirl in the infrared light of his sunglasses. He wriggles a little further into the ducting, the sound of his uncomfortable progress echoing along its dark length.

Further ahead, something retreats a little deeper into the darkness.

'I should warn you,' the Doctor calls out, with some difficulty, 'that I think I might be stuck.'

His voice reverberates in the gloom. Nothing and no one replies.

'Question,' says the Doctor, again with some difficulty. 'Forward or back?'

If you think the Doctor should try to go back, go to 36.

If you think he should carry on, go to 24.

22

The Doctor snatches up the electric guitar and slings the strap over his shoulder. He kicks on the amplifier with one foot, then bashes out a power chord at full volume.

The sound reverberates around the TARDIS. The Doctor loves it when he can feel the noise as well as hear it. He strikes a pose and plays the opening bars of 'Whole Lotta Love' by Led Zeppelin.

Something moves under his feet, startled by the thrilling grind of the music. It dashes around the power core, up the stairs and across the control room in a flurry of legs. The Doctor whirls, following its progress with the guitar's neck. The creature – he catches a glimpse of something insectoid, with many jointed legs – races for the open doors and shoots out of the TARDIS.

The guitar falls silent, leaving only an echoing hum on the verge of feedback. The TARDIS is quiet. The Doctor switches off the amp and crosses to the console. His fingers hesitate over the controls.

If you think the Doctor should close the TARDIS doors and leave, go to 32.

If you think he should follow the creature, go to 7.

23

'I want to talk to it first,' the Doctor tells Kate.

'It's a hostile alien life form, Doctor,' Kate argues. 'My orders are quite clear: terminate with maximum prejudice.'

'I *must* try to communicate with it first,' the Doctor insists. 'It's wounded, scared and a million light years from home. No wonder it's hostile. You would be too.'

'You don't look well enough to stand, let alone negotiate,' Kate observes.

'Let me worry about that.'

Kate sighs, then – clearly against what she feels is her better judgement – signals to the chopper pilot to take them down.

The creature is lying in the middle of some waste ground, tentacles quivering. The helicopter blades whip up a storm of litter as the Doctor climbs out of the aircraft and approaches the alien.

'Ready to talk?' the Doctor asks, swaying on his feet. He can feel the toxins from the creature's stings weakening him by the minute.

'*Keep away from me, Earth-thing!*'

'If I was from Earth, all of those stings would have killed me by now. But I'm in a bad way and, frankly, I need your help.'

'*I can't help you, Doctor.*'

'We can help each other.'

If you think the creature will help the Doctor, go to 86.

If you think the creature will refuse, go to 98.

24

The Doctor wriggles himself forward. There's not much room at all. He can barely move. Gritting his teeth, breathing hard, he squirms along the ducting inch by inch. *Or is it centimetre by centimetre in this era?* he wonders.

He brushes through a series of cobwebs, ducking to let the spiders run past. 'Keep out of my hair,' he tells them. 'I've got enough problems already.'

Up ahead, there is only deep darkness. But the Doctor knows there is something there. Something that keeps retreating, little by little, staying just far enough ahead of him to remain concealed in the shadows.

After a breathless wait in the darkness, something clangs up ahead and a dim orange light fills the duct. The creature has forced open another vent and escaped! Gritting his teeth, the Doctor wriggles faster. He reaches the vent and, with some degree of difficulty, clambers out into a large side room. The area is lit by sodium lamps – hence the orange light – but there is no sign of the creature.

The Doctor brushes spiderwebs and dust from his coat and trousers, noting that the only exit from the room is an antigravity lift shaft.

If you think the Doctor should take the lift shaft down, go to 104.

If you think he should take it up, go to 44.

25

The Doctor staggers to the TARDIS control console. He's weak and disorientated. Being in the TARDIS helps, but he needs an antidote quickly.

The creature crawls across the floor, dragging its tentacles. The stings leave a trail of poison behind them.

'I hope you're going to clean up after yourself,' the Doctor says, setting the controls for the moon where he found the creature.

'*Hurry!*' gasps the creature. '*I do not have long. And neither do you.*'

'Well, then we need each other. I'm hoping that means I can trust you.'

'*We shall see, Time Lord. A laboratory might provide a suitable antidote – but I must return to the cave system first.*'

The time rotors whirr and the TARDIS hurtles through the Vortex.

'The caves? Is that where you came from?' the Doctor asks.
'We never did get to the bottom of that.'

'*I have no recollection of my origins,*' the creature states. '*I exist.*'

'And you want to keep on existing?'

'*Every living thing does.*'

'All creatures great and small,' murmurs the Doctor. He
checks the controls and the scanner. 'We're nearly there. And
we have a choice: either land in the research lab, or in the
cave system beneath. Which is it to be?'

If you think the creature should choose the lab, go to 96.

If you think it should choose the caves, go to 121.

It takes more time than the Doctor expected. 'The control linkages are down and the calibrators are completely misaligned,' he grumbles as he works. He looks over the top of his sonic sunglasses at Eva, eyes bulging with anxiety. 'It's like working on the TARDIS.'

'Please hurry,' implores Eva. She is slumped in the machine. Her skin is growing more translucent by the second, as the malignocites in her bloodstream get to work.

The Doctor finishes a connection and slams the access hatch shut. He whips off his glasses and smiles at her. 'All done!'

'It took too long,' Eva gasps. 'I'm . . . going . . .'

'No, no, no!' The Doctor's long fingers dart over the controls and the machine hums to life. A bright field of sparkling energy envelops Eva, and a loud whining fills the air.

'C'mon, c'monnnn,' urges the Doctor.

The energy field disappears, the process complete. Eva lies in the sarcophagus, utterly immobile.

'Up you get,' says the Doctor, clicking his fingers. 'I can't stand dawdlers.'

Eva still doesn't move. The Doctor touches her face in sudden concern and finds it cold. Hurriedly he checks her pulse. There is none. Eva is dead.

'Too late,' he whispers fearfully. 'I was too late.'

With great gentleness, the Doctor closes Eva's eyes. He lowers his head in despair. A huge wave of helpless anger surges through him, rising up to blaze fiercely in his eyes. He turns his baleful glare on the calibration machine and strikes it hard with one bony fist. The clang echoes around the room like a church bell.

The Doctor jumps abruptly to his feet, his mind racing.

The laboratory – the whole research complex built on this

hellish moon – is now deserted, except for him. He could just leave. He could set the atmospheric controls to self-destruct, and obliterate the labs and the malignocites forever.

Or he could stay here and find whoever – or whatever – is responsible.

If you think the Doctor should destroy the entire research complex, go to 54.

If you think he should stay and find out who is responsible, go to 31.

27

The Doctor scans the rat with his sonic screwdriver. The result leaves no room for doubt

'I'm very sorry, Skid. The nanites are present in your bloodstream in very large numbers.'

The rat gives a sad squeak.

'Of course,' the Doctor says. 'I'll do my best to help. But I should warn you – I tried before with a human and it didn't work out well.'

The Doctor takes Skid to a workbench and switches on some of the equipment. 'This may take some time,' he warns. 'Each atomic cell machine is relatively simple, but in large numbers they can combine into fiendishly clever patterns. That's what causes the mutations.'

The Doctor peers at Skid's blood through a spectronic analyser. The rat sits patiently.

'I've learned a few things about the malignocites, though,'

the Doctor says. 'There's a chance that bombardment
with ultronic delta rays could cause the nanites to dissipate
harmlessly.'

Skid squeaks with alarm.

'What do you mean, "will that actually work"?' The Doctor
frowns at the rat. 'I mean, obviously there is an element of
risk, but . . .'

If you think the Doctor's machine will work, go to 47.

If you don't think it will work, go to 55.

28

The malignocite roars and charges. The Doctor dives out of the way, but a long pair of legs hook on to his jacket and wrench him back.

The jaws splay open, drooling long strings of foul-smelling saliva. The creature hauls the Doctor's struggling form closer to its great maw.

'You'll find me very indigestible,' the Doctor says. He pulls at his jacket but the material is caught fast in the creature's long legs. He quickly finds himself caught in a frantic, deadly tug of war.

'I'm over two thousand years old!' the Doctor complains. 'Well past my use-by date! Honestly, you'd be better off without me!'

The malignocite pulls on the Doctor's coat, hooking more legs deep into the cloth. The Doctor twists and turns and pulls, but is still dragged closer.

'I'll give you a terrible stomach upset,' he gasps, staring into the widening mouth. Glutinous acid bubbles within. 'Although, with digestive juices like that, I don't think a tummy ache is going to bother you much, is it?'

The Doctor weakens for a moment, as if accepting his fate.

Then, with a horrible tearing noise, he pulls free and hurtles across the lab.

'Look what you've done to my coat!' he protests.

Go to 37.

29

The Doctor follows Jiao through a series of airlocks, closing each behind them.

'Airlocks won't stop the nanite cloud,' he tells her, 'but they will slow it down.'

'How long have we got?'

'To live? Five minutes, if we're lucky.'

'Five minutes?'

The Doctor nods. 'Yes, five whole minutes. Three hundred seconds. Slightly less now. Let's say about two hundred and ninety.'

'You're very calm about it, I must say.'

'Well, you can do a lot in five minutes.'

'*Less* than five minutes.'

'Two hundred and eighty seconds.'

Jiao's lips form a thin, determined line. She matches the Doctor frown for frown. 'So what do we do? C'mon, let's make the most of our two hundred and eighty seconds.'

'Two hundred and seventy.'

'Whatevs.'

'I like you.'

'Shh,' Jiao holds up a hand. 'Listen.'

A humming noise is growing steadily louder, rising in pitch like the buzz of a thousand angry wasps.

'The nanite cloud,' whispers the Doctor.

'Already?'

'It's faster than I thought!'

'This way.' Jiao leads the Doctor through another, larger airlock. It takes time to cycle open and even longer to close behind them. The sound of the nanites is getting louder all the time.

'Two hundred and forty seconds,' says the Doctor helpfully. He aims the sonic at the locking mechanism as the nanite cloud appears on the other side of the airlock porthole, a swirling grey mass scratching at the plasteel. The sonic flashes bright blue and the locks hum into position.

'Two hundred and twenty-five seconds.'

'That's really not helping,' says Jiao. 'Can you stop it?'

'That depends on where we're going, and how long it's going to take to get there.'

'We're heading for the shuttle bay. There's a ship there – it's small, but it'll get us and any other survivors away from the moon.'

'Sounds like a plan,' the Doctor admits. 'But what if we don't want to get away from the moon?'

'Come again?'

'What's the alternative?'

Jiao shrugs. 'Head for the caves, I suppose.'

The Doctor considers this carefully.

If you think the Doctor should continue heading for the space shuttle, go to 84.

If you think he should head for the caves instead, go to 58.

30

'Doctor . . . it's getting worse.'

The Doctor looks up from his work. Eva is clearly in pain and her skin looks raw, as if it's fading from view.

'I'm being skinned alive!' she screams.

'No you're not,' the Doctor replies emphatically. 'The malignocites are breaking down the cells of your epidermis, molecule by molecule. The skin is still there, it's just transparent.'

Eva moans as she holds up her hands and sees the muscles and tendons exposed.

'We still have time,' the Doctor insists. 'We can do this!'

'Hurry!'

'You can't hurry genius!' The Doctor gives the machine a hefty whack with the flat of his hand and it hums into life. 'There!'

Eva collapses to the floor. The muscles that make up her

face are plainly visible, but even they are beginning to fade.
The Doctor can see veins and tendons pulsing in her neck.

Go to 107.

31

The Doctor gathers himself and searches the laboratory, ignoring the bodies of both Eva and the man. They are gone; there is nothing he can do for them now, except find what caused the infection and put it right.

A computer terminal yields to the glare of his sonic sunglasses, offering a full list of the research personnel and a schematic map of the base. Eva was the youngest scientist here, he notes sadly. A terrible waste.

It appears the malignocite research was carried out in the deepest part of the complex, located far below ground. The Doctor casts his eyes around the lab once more, and spots an antigravity tube. He floats down in it, all the way to the lowest level, where he forces the electronic lock on the access door and it hums open.

As he steps through, he's flooded by bright and sterile lighting.

The Doctor's boots echo as he walks across a wide chamber lined with glass-fronted modules. Each module contains a black rat in an increasingly advanced stage of malignocite infection: the first rat appears healthy, while the last is no more than a tiny skeleton.

If you think the Doctor should try to save the healthy rat, go to 13.

If you think he should continue his search for answers, go to 126.

32

The Doctor operates the door control and the TARDIS is sealed from the outside universe. Trimonic locks materialise into place and the time machine's interior suddenly exists in a separate dimension.

He doesn't set the controls to take-off just yet, though. Something, some instinct, makes him hesitate.

Something's wrong . . .

He still has the feeling that he isn't alone. The Doctor enjoys company, and he loves an audience, but this isn't right.

This is intrusive.

Threatening.

And it's locked in the TARDIS with him.

A very quiet rustling catches his attention, like something dry and withered moving for the first time.

Very slowly, the Doctor looks up from the complex hexagonal control console.

The time rotor – the series of giant cogs located directly above – is stationary.

It is also surrounded by shadows in which dark, unseen things move.

The shadows themselves begin to move.

The shadows *are* the dark, unseen things.

And now they are seen.

The Doctor's keen eyes adjust to the darkness, and his fingers reach for the sonic sunglasses. He has a feeling he'll be needing them. Strange creatures are clustered around the time rotor, like bats in a cave, huddled together for warmth.

Go to 119.

33

'There will be no time to do anything if we don't seal the cockpit first!' Garon insists.

The Doctor seals the cockpit door with his sonic screwdriver. The black cloud hisses angrily, effectively cut off. It won't be long before it finds a way in, though.

'Spacesuits, quickly!' the Doctor orders, pulling emergency survival suits out from the bulkhead storage lockers. 'Everyone, put one on!'

He hands a suit to Jiao and throws the rest of the suits to the remaining crew. After a brief hesitation, which the Doctor overrides with one of his fiercest frowns, they all climb into the thin but super-strong steelex spacesuits.

'Are we going on a spacewalk?' asks Jiao, her voice muffled by the helmet.

'Sort of,' the Doctor tells her. 'More of a space dive, to be honest.'

'But you don't have a spacesuit!'

'Not enough to go round. I'll be OK. Now jump!'

'This is madness,' objects the pilot.

'No time to argue!' The Doctor thumps the emergency cockpit-release control and the transpex canopy is blown away, whipping back into the atmosphere. The shuttle instantly veers out of control, buffeted by the thin winds of the moon's barren surface.

The occupants of the flight cabin are all sucked out into the void – or so it seems. They are near enough to the moon's surface to be caught in its feeble gravity, and gently float downwards as the shuttle careers into the surface. The ship explodes in a mighty orange fireball, and a great spray of rocks and dust is thrown into the air.

Jiao drifts slowly down, trying to keep track of where her friends and colleagues are as they head towards the surface. She feels a desperate sense of loss at the thought of the poor souls who were trapped with the nanite cloud on the shuttle.

A long, thin figure swoops past her, coat tails flapping in the breeze of his descent. The Doctor's grey hair is pulled back from his high forehead, deep-set eyes ablaze with determination. *This is a man,* Jiao realises, *who enjoys surviving against all odds.*

The Doctor spreads his arms, adjusting the course of his flight, and aims towards a particular spot on the moon's surface.

Go to 68.

34

The Doctor makes his way into the cave. It's dark but he can just make out the hard, craggy walls and uneven, pockmarked ground. Loose stones crunch beneath his boots as he creeps forward. The sound echoes like gunshots through the cave.

He heads down deeper, to where the shadows are darkest and coldest. Lichen grows in scabby blotches across the rock, glowing with a dim, sickly light. He can only just make out the way ahead, festooned with thick, stringy cobwebs.

Eventually he hears a sound in the distance – not the reverberation of his scuffling footsteps, but something altogether more sinister: voices.

They are not human voices.

The sounds they make are guttural and animalistic, but there is a rhythm, almost a chant. The desperate, alien cry does nothing to soothe the Doctor's nerves.

If you think the Doctor should follow the voices, go to 106.

If you think he should retreat, go to 75.

35

The Doctor stands his ground as the giant malignocite approaches.

More legs unfold from beneath the great insectoid torso, and massive jaws flex around the rows of jagged black teeth. A low, irregular hissing brings forth a dreadful stench from the depths of its thorax.

'Do I know you?' wonders the Doctor, frowning.

The creature hisses like a gas main about to explode. The Doctor's frown deepens and his eyes burn with curiosity.

'I *do* know you, don't I?' he realises happily. 'It's Eva, isn't it? Och, I knew you when you were only so high and blonde. And human, of course . . . something which seems to have been largely forgotten in your new form.'

The malignocite's jaws quiver and dark slime drools from its mandibles as they flex like giant fingers grasping for the Doctor's head.

The Doctor ducks back. 'It's me! The Doctor! I tried to save you, remember?' The Doctor gives an apologetic shrug. 'Didn't quite come off, I'll admit, but it's the thought that counts . . . isn't it?'

The malignocite lets out another ferocious hiss.

If you think the malignocite is trying to communicate with the Doctor, go to 40.

If you think the malignocite is going to attack, go to 28.

36

'This is ridiculous,' grumbles the Doctor, wriggling backwards.

He stops. He's not moving; not even an inch. Or a centimetre. Or a glrnk.

He tries wriggling forward, but there is no progress that way either.

'Inevitable conclusion: I'm stuck.'

The Doctor never panics. He is not inclined to panic. Panic is pointless and usually counterproductive. At times like this you need a clear head and a logical plan of action.

At times like this . . .

The Doctor can't remember a time when he was physically stuck anywhere. Prison cells, parallel dimensions, time loops . . . but never a ventilation shaft. How embarrassing.

'This is ridiculous,' he repeats. His voice echoes along the shaft. 'I'm thin. Very thin. I have seldom been thinner.

Perhaps during my tenth incarnation, but it's touch-and-go.'

He sighs, although it is not easy when trapped in a ventilation shaft. 'The problem is too much touch and not enough go,' he reflects miserably.

Something else, however, is moving very easily in the shaft. Something dark and clawed and hostile.

The Doctor stares at it.

It's coming straight for him.

Go to 64.

37

The Doctor runs for his life. He can hear the sound of pursuit behind him – ferocious and hungry.

He reaches the end of the corridor and aims his sonic screwdriver at the controls of the antigravity lift shaft located there. The open shaft fills with antigravity beams and he leaps into them, buoyed aloft in an instant.

At the base of the shaft dwindling beneath him, he sees the creature struggling through the opening. If it gets into the shaft, the same antigravity beams will carry it straight up after the Doctor.

But he has an idea.

Reaching the top of the antigravity shaft, the Doctor climbs on to the highest level and uses the sonic on the shaft controls.

'Reversing the polarity!' he yells triumphantly. 'Never fails!'

The hum of the antigravity beams changes to a sudden roar as their direction is reversed, and the malignocite is pulled suddenly down the shaft at a tremendous speed. The Doctor winces as the creature hits the bottom with a loud crunch.

The antigravity beams continue to roar and the remains of the creature are slowly flattened into a slimy puddle.

'This is where a lesser man would make a joke about the gravity of the situation,' the Doctor notes sadly. He turns away from the shaft and frowns. The antigravity beams are still in reverse. The Doctor tries to switch them off but the controls are fused. The roar is loud enough to shake the building now.

'Oh, this isn't good,' he mutters, looking quickly around the lab. He's a long way from the main atmospheric control systems now. There's no way to override the antigravity beam. It's still trying to pull everything down – including the rest of the lab complex.

'Now I *am* beginning to see the gravity of the situation.' The Doctor sighs.

The lab starts to collapse around him. He staggers across to the TARDIS and hurries inside. A loud wheezing, groaning sound fills the air, and the old police box fades quickly away, just before the research lab crumples like an old paper bag and disappears in a brilliant explosion.

THE END

38

'I like a warm reception as much as the next man,' says the Doctor. 'But a flamethrower?'

The woman looks down at the gun in her hand, and then back at the Doctor. But he's already dived back down the antigravity shaft.

It's a longer drop than he thought, and the gravity compensators aren't ready for someone just throwing themselves into the shaft.

He spreadeagles like a skydiver to make it a bit easier for the G-fields.

Eventually, coat tails streaming out behind him like madly flailing wings, the Doctor's descent slows. He floats past the level he came in on and carries on down . . .

After a few seconds he realises he's fallen the entire length of the lab complex and is now effectively underground – and still dropping.

He swiftly becomes aware that the bottom of the shaft is approaching rather more rapidly than he would prefer. At this speed, the impact will break every bone in his body and turn his brains into soup.

He fishes out the sonic and fires it at the control filament running down the length of the shaft. The gravity compensators whine and he slows to a halt, boots lightly touching the concrete floor.

Go to 57.

39

The Doctor scans the rat with his sonic glasses. 'Don't worry, it won't hurt. I just want to check for nanites.' He has recalibrated the glasses to detect the presence of malignocites.

'Congratulations,' the Doctor tells Skid when he's done, removing the glasses. 'You're perfectly healthy. You've got months ahead of you. Maybe even a year or more.'

Skid squeals and runs round to the Doctor's other shoulder. 'What's up, rat? What's spooking you?' Skid starts again and the Doctor closes his eyes, concentrating. 'Changes? New rats? Bad rats. Not rats . . . I'm not sure I understand, Skid.'

And then the Doctor opens his eyes and sees what's in the other modules – the ones that contain rodent skeletons. The tiny bones twitch and curl, writhing like maggots, and then suddenly darken and swell and sprout new, stiff little limbs.

The Doctor's frown deepens as the creatures grow in their cages with a sound like popping knuckles. More legs extend from the glistening new bodies, pressing and scratching against the glass as the hideous forms mutate out of the remains of the rats.

'It's happening all over the lab,' realises the Doctor in horror. 'Which means it must be happening all over the research base!'

Go to 42.

40

The malignocite closes in on the Doctor, its fangs inches from his neck.

'I really think you need to reconsider this,' says the Doctor, speaking quickly and urgently. He stares straight into the dark orbs clustered at the centre of the malignocite's bulbous head. 'Surely there's some trace of your humanity left in there?'

The creature stares back at him, dark eyes bulging unnaturally, as if the alien brain inside is trying to focus on the strange, forgotten shape before it.

'It's me! The Doctor! And you're Eva! I know it's you . . . the nanites have run riot through your DNA and *changed* you.' The Doctor's face falls a little. 'I have to say, Eva, it's not a good look.'

The malignocite seems to hesitate.

The Doctor thinks he's getting through. 'Eva – if you can hear me, if you can understand me, then give me a sign.'

The malignocite falls silent, seeming to focus its gaze on the Doctor.

'Anything . . .'

The Doctor stares into the alien eyes and searches out unknowable thoughts . . . but he finds nothing. There is no sign of the human being he knew.

'Oh, Eva, you are lost,' the Doctor admits.

Go to 48.

41

The Doctor crawls out of the swirling dust. Behind him flames crackle in the wreckage. He drags himself with bloodied hands along the ground towards the shelter of a cave. Inside is the entrance to a lift shaft, one that uses antigravity rays. It could be a way out.

Black smoke coils in the air around him. It takes him a few seconds to realise that the smoke is behaving very oddly. Instead of just floating around willy-nilly, it seems to be moving purposefully, like a swarm of bees.

It's buzzing too.

The Doctor's eyes widen as he realises it's the nanite cloud. It's survived the crash of the shuttle – just like he has.

As the humming cloud drifts closer, the Doctor staggers to his feet, dizzy and confused. He thinks he's hallucinating: the cloud is condensing into a solid black shape.

As he watches, the nanite cloud draws itself together into

one solid being. Each tiny particle joins to the next, and the next, in a continuous construction. The result is a two-metre-high two-legged creature of glistening black scales and a knot of bulging eyes above an eel-like mouth. It reaches out with long, sinuous arms towards the Doctor. Each arm ends in a cluster of flexing hooks sharp enough to shred flesh.

The Doctor backs slowly away. His head is still spinning. The creature lumbers after him. It's not particularly quick, but the Doctor is convinced that it will not tire – it is, after all, formed from a billion microscopic machines all joined together. 'Not unlike any living creature, really,' he thinks aloud. 'Machines instead of cells. Extraordinary – but deadly.'

He soon realises there are only two ways he can go: into a dark tunnel leading deeper into the cave system where he might be able to hide, or he could trust himself to the antigravity lift shaft.

If you think the Doctor should use the antigravity lift shaft, go to 59.

If you think he should take the cave tunnel, go to 34.

42

The Doctor backs slowly away from the mutating rat corpses. Skid mewls in alarm.

The Doctor slips on his sonic sunglasses for a closer look at the mutants. Some are so big they fill the glass modules, their angular black legs scraping at the edges, probing for a weak spot.

'If I didn't know better, I'd say the malignocites have broken down the original genetic structure and rebuilt it to their own design.' The Doctor turns to look at Skid. 'In other words, giant malignocites!'

Something crashes through the lab door in a skittering tangle of black legs. Skid bolts off the Doctor's shoulder in terror. The creature towers over the Doctor, its long, sinuous body stooping under the low ceiling. A flattened head opens into a wide, distended jaw full of drooling black fangs.

'Have you considered using mouthwash?' asks the Doctor, recoiling from its oily breath.

The creature advances towards the Doctor, hissing angrily.

If you think the Doctor should confront the giant malignocite, go to 35.

If you think he should look for a quick exit, go to 28.

43

The Doctor considers his options carefully. He could remove the Time Vector Generator, but then the interior of the TARDIS will collapse to the size of an ordinary police box. It might flush the monsters out, but it will also flush him out. And then what?

There has to be another way.

The Doctor doesn't want to give up his TARDIS that easily.

Very carefully he begins to sidle round the edge of the TARDIS control room. The creatures on the ceiling are getting agitated, flexing long, multijointed legs like a cluster of dark moths about to hatch.

If he can reach the central console, or even one of the control stations on the perimeter of the flight deck, he might be able to take off in the TARDIS while leaving the creatures behind. It's a lot easier to materialise the TARDIS *around* something, though . . .

The Doctor reaches for a control lever just as the creatures finally stir.

Several drop down from the ceiling with a clatter and angry snarls. They glare murderously at the Doctor, who stands frozen at the controls.

Then they leap towards him.

The Doctor whirls and dives for the nearest exit.

Go to 63.

44

The Doctor peers up the lift shaft, craning his neck to see how far it goes.

'Well, it is an *anti*gravity shaft,' he remarks. He presses the ASCEND control and steps into the open shaft. Antigravity beams carry him aloft. He rises up the shaft at a steady rate, passing level after level.

'Always go straight to the top,' he reminds himself, hands nonchalantly in pockets as he waits to reach the highest level. Eventually he steps out on to a wide platform under a transparent domed ceiling. Stars shine brightly above him and around him.

'Hello,' he says, addressing the tall woman he finds waiting on the platform. She's dressed in grubby overalls with her red hair tied up. Her eyes are fierce, her lips thin. She's pointing some kind of weapon straight at the Doctor.

'Keep back!' she yells. 'I'll fire! I swear to the stars, I'll roast you where you stand if you come any closer!'

She looks serious. Terrified, in fact. She could do anything. Her finger is already tightening on the trigger.

If you think the Doctor should jump back down the antigravity shaft, go to 38.

If you think he should stay and face the woman with the gun, go to 50.

'Can we talk about this?' asks the Doctor. 'Just the two of us? And I don't mean Kate and me. I mean *you* and me.'

Kate stares back at him, uncertain. 'What are you talking about?'

'Come on, you must've picked up a smattering of English while you were in my mind,' the Doctor says, still addressing the creature. 'I know you can understand me. Let's talk.'

The knuckles of Kate's hand are white on the handgrip of the gun but the muzzle doesn't waver. 'Doctor, I'm warning you . . .'

'Shh,' says the Doctor, putting a finger to his lips. 'You're looking out through my eyes; you can talk through my mouth.'

'*There is . . . nothing to . . . discuss.*' The voice is cold, alien, almost clammy. It's as if the creature is struggling to control the Doctor's lips.

'Rubbish,' the Doctor says, regaining control. 'There's always something to talk about, even if it's only the price of fish. Or how odd it feels to have a conversation with yourself while an alien creature controls your voice.'

'*You will be . . . eradicated. You will all be . . . eradicated.*'

'Or,' the Doctor says, 'we could talk about that.'

'*You will be eradicated!*' This time the words are harsh and forceful, bringing spittle to the corners of the Doctor's mouth.

'I'm confused,' says Kate. 'Stop talking like that or I *will* shoot you.'

The Doctor sighs. 'Maybe you're right. Maybe there isn't anything to discuss after all.'

'I've heard enough,' Kate says.

Go to 123.

46

'This way,' says the Doctor, pulling Eva through a door marked BASEMENT. 'We don't have time for the shuttle.'

'There's a good chance we'll be trapped in there, though.'

'It'll give me time to think,' the Doctor says, letting the door hiss shut behind them. He hits the lock switch. 'The door is airtight. The nanite cloud can't get through.'

The dark cloud swirls against the porthole set into the door. The mist looks busy and hostile, almost intelligent.

'At least let's hope it doesn't think of a way through,' the Doctor says, heading for the stairs.

'Could it do that?'

'I've no idea. It's an entirely new life form – if it's even alive in any sense we can understand. At the moment it's just a sort of hive mind – one single being made up of thousands of individuals.'

They hurry down the stairs, flight after flight, their footsteps echoing off the metallic walls.

'What's down here anyway?' asks the Doctor.

'Basic life-support systems, energy stacks, that kind of thing.'

A loud clang echoes down the stairwell.

'What was that?' Eva whispers.

'Something breaking through the airtight door.'

'The nanite cloud?'

'It's not a cloud any more. The nanomachines have united to form a single entity.'

Go to 127.

47

'What are ultronic delta rays? Something I've just invented, actually. But they'll work, I'm sure.' Crossing his fingers for luck, the Doctor activates the spectron-ray machine. Skid is bathed in pulsating green light.

'I think it's working, Skid! Hang on to your tail, sunshine – this is going to be marvellous!'

The green light reaches maximum brilliance, almost blindingly bright. When it fades, Skid is left on the dais looking exhausted but unharmed.

'Please tell me you're all right,' says the Doctor.

The rat squeaks.

'Well, good,' says the Doctor, 'because according to these readings the nanites have all gone. No ill effects? No dizziness? No headaches, vomiting or unsightly rashes?'

The rat squeaks again.

'Then I declare that a win,' the Doctor announces. He

aims his sonic screwdriver and sets a program running on the spectron-ray machine. 'That'll send a waveform through the entire base, neutralising every nanite it finds. Anyone else unlucky enough to come to this moon will be quite safe.'

The rat squeaks at him.

'Yes, I know. It's time for me to go. But I can't leave you here all on your own, can I?' The Doctor's eyes twinkle. 'Fancy a quick trip in my time machine?'

THE END

48

The Doctor dives towards the nearest doorway. The malignocite roars and crashes in pursuit, throwing everything aside in its ferocious haste to catch him.

The Doctor slides to a halt at the door, landing on his knees. It's locked. His fingers scrabble at the controls, but to no avail.

The creature is right behind him.

'Wait!' cries the Doctor, whirling round. He holds up his hand towards the malignocite and, remarkably, the creature pauses for a moment.

The malignocite growls.

In the Doctor's hand is a lollipop.

He pulled it, to his own great surprise, from his jacket pocket. He'd forgotten it was there.

'You might enjoy this,' the Doctor says, holding the lollipop out a little further. The malignocite's eyes bulge and focus on the sweet.

'It's a wee bit fluffy,' apologises the Doctor. 'But –'

A long, thin tentacle shoots out of the creature's mouth and snaps up the lollipop.

The Doctor turns, digs in his pocket for his sonic screwdriver, and aims it at the door, praying for the lock to click open.

If you think the door will open in time, go to 37.

If you think it will stay locked, go to 51.

49

Fighting against the thing that is claiming his mind, the Doctor reaches with desperate hope for the telepathic circuits. If he can pilot the TARDIS subconsciously, perhaps he can avoid surrendering to the will of the alien creature on his back.

He plunges his long fingers deep into the soft membranes of the control console's telepathic interface. The creature, sensing immediate treachery, grips harder and the Doctor sinks to his knees with a groan.

He keeps contact with the telepathic circuits and, through them, the TARDIS itself.

The time machine responds to his subconscious mind, tuning into something not even the Doctor is aware of, and bypassing, he fervently hopes, the menacing passenger clinging to both his back and his brain.

The time rotor whirrs, the TARDIS engines heave, and the familiar wheezing and grinding echoes through the ship.

Materialisation is seconds away.

The Doctor collapses to the floor.

The TARDIS has not travelled far. He can sense that, at least. And so can the creature on his back. It moves nervously, gripping him more tightly, thin antennae quivering.

'What are you?' gasps the Doctor.

He activates the door control and crawls towards the exit.

Go to 125.

50

'Just what do you think you're doing?' the Doctor asks, eyes blazing.

The woman is momentarily startled. 'What?'

'Yes! *What.* Exactly that.' The Doctor's eyebrows draw together and he fixes the woman with a ferocious stare. Before she can react, he's stepped forward and taken the weapon out of her hands.

'Give that back!' she says, reaching for it.

'I don't think so,' the Doctor says, holding it easily out of reach. 'Not until I know who *you* are, and that you know it would be a terrible mistake to kill me. Or anybody, for that matter.'

She slumps down into a nearby chair and runs a hand over her face. She's clearly exhausted. 'I don't make a habit of trying to kill people,' she explains. 'My name is Penny. Chief scientist, Research Base Twelve.'

'I'm the Doctor. Tell me what happened.'

'We were working on the malignocite programme –'

'Malignocite?'

'Genetically engineered biomechs that can strip living matter from enemy facilities and leave the structures and hardware intact.'

The Doctor frowns. 'Small, dark and insectoid? I think I met one.'

'You're lucky to be alive then. They've killed everyone else. The programme was nearing its conclusion. One of the junior technicians made a mistake and the first batch of malignocites got free. They ate through the rest of the staff in less than a day. I managed to get up here to the viewing platform. There's only one way in here: the antigravity shaft. Anything that comes up from down below gets blasted by that flamethrower.'

'And what's the long-term plan?'

Penny shrugs. 'There isn't one. I can't go anywhere. I'll starve to death eventually. Or fall asleep, and the malignocites will get me then.'

'How many malignocites are there?'

'The first batch contained about four hundred.'

'And how many staff have lost their lives?'

'There were twelve of us.'

'Right,' says the Doctor. 'I'll get round to who to blame later. But for now survival is everything. It's time to fight back.'

Go to 113.

51

The door refuses to unlock.

The sonic screwdriver's blue light flickers busily but without result.

'Deadlocked,' grunts the Doctor unhappily.

Behind him, the creature coughs and growls threateningly. The Doctor switches off the sonic and carefully returns it to his inside pocket. Then he turns and straightens up, brushing his jacket lapels smooth before looking the monster square in the eyes.

'So what's it to be?' the Doctor asks. 'Bite my head off? Suck out my brains? Skin me alive?'

The creature coughs again.

'You should get that looked at. What you need is a doctor.'

The creature coughs again, spluttering alien phlegm.

'Charming.'

Then the creature starts to choke, clutching at its throat

with its outsize claws, its multiple eyes bulging horribly.

'Actually, you don't look at all well . . . I mean, even worse than before,' the Doctor notes with a frown.

The creature staggers back, still choking, and the Doctor suddenly realises what's wrong.

'You've swallowed the lollipop! Oh, you foolish monster! You're only supposed to lick it. It would've lasted longer!'

The creature turns and dives into the ventilator-shaft ducting, scrambling quickly out of view.

'Wait!' The Doctor hurries after it. 'Come back!'

Go to 21.

52

'I can't keep it any longer,' the Doctor says, his voice ragged with the strain. 'I have to reject it!'

He clutches his head as if he wants to stop it from exploding. That would be too horrible – Kate would never get the stains out of her coat for one thing, and where would he be without any brains? Would he regenerate? Would he transform into a mindless zombie-Doctor?

He is losing all sense of who he is. The parasite has sensed that its host is trying to reject it and focuses all of its energy on keeping the Doctor under control. But the Doctor will not be controlled. His mind will not be controlled by a genetically engineered insect!

With a final, anguished cry the Doctor forces the intruder from his consciousness. With a shrill squeal, the creature becomes visible and scrambles off the Doctor's back and neck, raking its sharp claws across his scalp.

The thing falls to the ground and squirms madly.

The Doctor sinks to his knees, exhausted.

'Be careful,' he warns Kate – but it's too late.

The creature has already leaped on to her back!

Go to 110.

53

The Doctor and Jiao race through the nearest door. The black cloud stirs and begins to follow.

'It's coming after us!' Jiao cries.

The Doctor turns and points his sonic screwdriver at the door control. The sonic pulses blue and the door slides shut, locks humming into place.

'Thank goodness!' Jiao gives a sigh of relief. 'Anything that gadget can't do?'

'It can't save us from that nanite cloud.'

'Nanite cloud?'

'The malignocites no longer need a living bloodstream to function. They've absorbed all the proteins and amino acids they need to form a cohesive multi-particle organism of their own.'

'A sort of combined life form, you mean?'

The Doctor nods grimly. 'Airborne death. Charming. I'd

like to meet whoever invented it.'

'You can. The surviving scientists are in the outer section of the base. I came back to see if anyone else was still alive.'

'Brave.'

'Stupid. We should have all abandoned base at the first hint of trouble.'

'True. And if we find your friends now, we could lead the nanite cloud straight to them. Can we take that risk?'

'What choice do we have?' Jiao insists, looking through the door's porthole window. 'That cloud's right outside and it looks like it's trying to interface with the door controls!'

Go to 29.

54

A long, loud roar reverberates through the lab complex. The Doctor activates a bank of CCTV screens and checks the images. There's something large and bestial working its way through the corridors towards him.

He uses the scanners to run a check on the creature. He can't see it clearly, but he has a nasty suspicion about what it could be. The computers process the data from the scans and project a complicated DNA schematic as a hologram.

'Just as I thought,' he growls disapprovingly. The malignocites were converting their victims into simulacra of themselves: full-size versions of each nanomachine. There were millions of malignocites in each human corpse: if they all found the right organic resources and energy, they would form a billion-strong army of these huge, deadly creatures.

The creature is nearly at the airlock. He can hear claws scrabbling at the metal-and-plastic seal.

He looks quickly around for a means to destroy it – or destroy the lab complex. He can't afford to leave these creatures to duplicate and escape from the moon. He can't see any self-destruct mechanism, though.

The creature is now pushing its way into the lab.

The Doctor has to get out.

Go to 37.

55

'Ultronic delta rays are something I've just invented,' the Doctor admits, 'but I promise you they'll work.'

Crossing his fingers for luck, the Doctor starts the spectron-ray machine and Skid is bathed in pulsating green light.

It doesn't go well . . .

Skid squeals loudly, arching his back, curling in on himself with an audible popping of muscles and ligaments.

'Well that's not right,' the Doctor says. He tries to shut the machine down, but it won't respond.

Skid screams and his fur turns hard and spiny as his body begins to swell. The rat throws back his head, opening huge jaws to show elongating teeth in multiple rows.

The Doctor aims his sonic screwdriver at the machine but it's now out of control.

Skid roars, doubling in size with a horrible sound of tearing meat and bone.

'This isn't what I planned at all,' the Doctor assures the rat. But Skid is no longer anything like a rat.

The Doctor backs away slowly, eyeing the exits. He can see two options: the lift, which is nearest, or a closed door on the far side of the room.

If you think the Doctor should head for the lift, go to 44.

If you think he should head for the door, go to 122.

DOCTOR WHO · CHOOSE THE FUTURE

56

The TARDIS spins through the Vortex like a leaf in a storm.

The Doctor is weakened but free. The creature has given up trying to control him and scuttled off to a far corner of the control room to lie in wait. It shivers and clicks in annoyance.

'We're travelling through time and space,' the Doctor tells it. 'If you're interested, that is. Are you interested? I can't tell. All I know is that you want to dominate my mind with every fibre of your being.'

The Doctor's hands play across the flight controls.

'In fact, you want to dominate the mind of any living creature you come across. That's how you live – by devouring the unique brainwaves of intelligent beings. I got that loud and clear when you got your hooks into mine. Well, I can't allow that to happen again. You're just a nightmare experiment gone horribly wrong.'

The creature hisses evilly.

'Don't take it to heart,' the Doctor says. 'We all have our bad days.'

The TARDIS lands with a familiar wheeze. The Doctor operates the door control. 'End of the line,' he tells the creature. 'Hop it.'

The creature slithers up the ramp that leads to the exit. It pauses on the threshold and glares at the Doctor.

'Don't bother trying to make me feel sorry for you,' the Doctor says coldly. 'It's not going to happen.'

The creature crawls out of the TARDIS into a brilliant white light.

'Stasis Point,' explains the Doctor, framed in the doorway. 'No space, no time. Most importantly, no intelligent life forms for you to control. The Shadow Proclamation uses these voids as prison cells for beings who are awaiting trial. I'll notify them that you're here. They'll get round to you in a couple of centuries.'

The creature, suspended in the white space, glares back.

'It's the best I can do,' says the Doctor, and he closes the TARDIS door.

He walks slowly back to the console and dematerialises the ship. He wishes there was someone else here. He wishes he could go back to the moon, go back to the beginning, and start again.

He thinks about it carefully . . .

THE END

57

Storage rooms, garages and passageways fill the basement. Dim electric lights are suspended at intervals along the walls.

The Doctor moves quickly, his boots echoing on the concrete. It's apparent that no one has been here for a very long time. The dust is thick on the cables and pipework, and dark cobwebs hang in rags from the light fittings.

But then the Doctor finds something rather disturbing.

In one of the furthest storage rooms, hooks line the walls and ceilings, and what appear to be bodies are hanging from the hooks.

Closer examination, however, reveals that the bodies are empty spacesuits. The material is cracked and worn. It looks like they've not been used for many years, far longer than the contents of the rest of the storeroom. Cockroaches roam in and out of the empty space helmets.

The atmosphere down here is all wrong, the Doctor thinks to himself.

There is a narrow door at the back of the room. It starts to open with a creak . . .

If you think the Doctor should find somewhere to hide, go to 112.

If you think he should wait and see who it is, go to 79.

58

'There's a cave system under the lab complex,' Jiao explains. 'We might be able to give it the slip down there.'

'That sounds just the thing,' says the Doctor. 'Lead on.'

Jiao takes him down to the basement. There they find an old metal staircase leading from the storage bay to the cave system below. It's cold and dank. The sound of dripping water echoes in the distance. They follow the narrow cave passageway deeper into the darkness.

'It's easy to get lost down here,' Jiao says.

'That I can believe. What I can't believe is the stupidity of human scientists inventing a nanite programme like the malignocites. You might as well write a suicide note saying "I'm a stupid human scientist – kill me now".'

'That's a little harsh.'

'So is being dissolved by a horde of microscopic machines. Heaven knows what they'll grow into. They might all join up to form one big monster. Wouldn't that be fun?'

They reach a fork in the tunnels.

'There's a lift along here that leads to the outer labs,' Jiao says. 'From there we could get to the escape shuttle.'

She hurries towards the lift, but the Doctor hesitates before following her. He knows that he has a tendency to attract trouble . . . Perhaps it would be safer for Jiao if he went his own way?

If you think the Doctor should continue alone, go to 34.

If you think the Doctor should stay with Jiao, go to 84.

59

The Doctor hurries towards the antigravity shaft. He's disappointed to find that the machinery is broken. It doesn't take a master technician to see that a piece of shuttle wreckage has completely destroyed the gravity compensators.

Frowning, the Doctor considers his options.

It appears he has none.

The creature – made from a million nanomachines – is striding towards him. It steps easily over the rubble and twisted metal, and looms out of the smoke. Its eyes are glowing.

The Doctor moves his frown up a notch from fuming to furious.

The monster growls, long and low, like a very hungry lion.

'There's only one thing for it,' the Doctor announces. Looking up, he can see the shaft is still negotiable. 'I've still got arms and legs, after all. Up and at it, Doctor!'

He clambers up the worst of the wreckage and gains a foothold at the bottom of the shaft. It's not an easy climb, but he is spurred on by the two fiercely glowing eyes regarding him with undisguised hatred from below.

Quicker than he would have thought possible, the Doctor ascends to the first level. He can see a set of controls! The machinery here is in perfect working order!

Go to 44.

60

The Doctor turns and runs. He doesn't want to put Kate – or any other human being – in danger.

'Stop!' Kate calls after him. 'Doctor, wait!'

A narrow path leads away from the TARDIS and Kate. The Doctor follows it, but he can hear Kate running after him, calling him. He has to get away.

Railway tracks run along a wide trench. Even the sight of a railway fails to lift the Doctor's spirits. He has to get rid of the creature on his back soon or it will devour him.

There's a train approaching – an express, travelling at around 150 miles per hour.

The Doctor can hear Kate behind him. He has to get away! He wonders for a moment if he should cross the tracks or not. The train is getting closer, and an idea is forming in his head. He feels the creature on his back writhe in concern and the Doctor allows himself a grim smile.

But Kate has caught up. She's drawn her UNIT-issue semi-automatic. The Doctor looks back at her with haunted eyes as the train bears down.

'Stop, or I'll shoot,' Kate warns, cocking the pistol.

If you think the Doctor should try to reason with the creature, go to 45.

If you think he should try to get away instead, go to 65.

61

'I want to stay in here,' Eva says. 'Where I'm safe.'

The Doctor regards her sadly. His eyes are full of an ancient, unknowable pain. 'Nowhere is truly safe,' he tells her. 'The nanites in your bloodstream are extremely advanced.'

He pushes one of the TARDIS scanner screens round to face Eva. On it is an image of her – and a diagram of the nanomachines in her blood.

'The malignocites are communicating with each other,' explains the Doctor. 'They're coming up with a plan, a way to defeat the TARDIS.'

Eva looks confused. 'Am I going to . . . die?'

'You're going to change.'

'Isn't there anything you can do to stop it?'

'I'm very sorry. I thought being inside the TARDIS would halt the process – but the nanites are too clever, and too determined.'

Eva suddenly coughs, doubling over in obvious pain. 'Oh no . . . What's happening?'

'The malignocites are rewriting your DNA. They've come up with a plan and now they're acting on it.'

Eva gasps and falls to her knees. Her skin blackens and hardens, her hands curling into claws and her back arching and sprouting sharp, blade-like ridges along her spine.

'It's a full-body metamorphosis,' says the Doctor. He watches in fascination and checks the diagnostic scanner again. 'The next stage will be radical cell mitosis – automatic reproduction. Things could be about to get very crowded in here!'

Eva's head splits in two, and her body follows it. The halves separate, flopping apart and squirming on the decking like giant, newborn tadpoles. Each half squeals and the two pieces separate into four.

Minutes later there are eight giant malignocites squealing on the TARDIS floor. They climb slowly to their clawed feet, blinking up at the Doctor with pulsating black eyes.

Then the malignocites turn and run, falling over each other in a hurry to get away.

'No, wait!' the Doctor shouts.

But it's too late. The creatures scramble up the TARDIS walls, dislodging books and keepsakes from the bookshelves, and swarm across the ceiling.

Go to 43.

62

The Doctor struggles feebly as the UNIT soldiers bundle him into a helicopter. The rotors thud loudly overhead and the aircraft lifts off.

'You should have left me,' the Doctor says as the chopper swings away from the scene.

'Rubbish,' Kate yells back over the roar of the rotors. 'Now stop complaining or I'll shove an aspirin down you and be done with it.'

'I thought I was a goner,' the Doctor confesses.

'Never mind that now. We're tracking the alien. If we're lucky, we'll get a clear shot.'

Looking out of the cockpit, the Doctor sees that the helicopter is following the alien across the railyards. It's using its tentacles to drag itself away from the battle.

'It's wounded,' he says. 'Crawling away to die.'

'We're going to make sure it does.'

The chopper swoops down towards the creature.

'We're armed with air-to-surface LionFang missiles,' Kate explains. 'They'll leave nothing but a crater. Say goodbye if you want to.'

'I might want to talk to it first.'

'It's a malignant alien parasite you brought to Earth. I'm not taking any chances.'

If you think Kate should fire the missiles now, go to 77.

If you think the Doctor should try to talk to the creature first, go to 23.

The Doctor races away from the TARDIS control room. *It's a desperate ploy, but it just might work*, he thinks. 'If only I could figure out what the ploy is,' he mutters.

He turns at the next intersection. The TARDIS is full of corridors and rooms and all kinds of places – in all his years, the Doctor has never fully explored it. There's too much to see in the rest of time and space, let alone in the time and space contained in his own ship.

He can hear the creatures rushing after him. Their insect-like legs clatter and scratch as they hurtle along the corridors.

The Doctor skids to a halt and dives through a pair of large double doors that lead to . . . a wardrobe.

But not just any wardrobe. This is huge. This is made from relative dimensions, just like the rest of the TARDIS. It's full of clothes of every kind, from every era, all dumped in piles or hanging on racks. He races up a spiral staircase, trips over an immensely long multicoloured scarf, and lands face down in a pile of folded cricket sweaters.

The creatures swarm after him. Cloaks, jackets and trousers fly everywhere.

The Doctor crawls out on all fours, an old black astrakhan hat perched on his head.

The creatures see him and hurtle in pursuit.

The Doctor slides down a fireman's pole that has been installed, for some unknown reason, in the wardrobe room. It leads through a hole in the floor straight into the library.

At the bottom he jumps off and races between two rows of high bookshelves. 'That reminds me,' he says aloud, 'I've a copy of *Through the Looking-Glass* that's well overdue!'

The monsters tear through the library after him, scraps of paper flying in their wake.

The Doctor turns left, right, doubles back and runs up a

ladder to the mezzanine level, before hurrying through non-fiction. 'Everyone hurries through non-fiction,' he remarks.

He runs out of the library into another corridor intersection and realises that he is, in fact, now lost in his own TARDIS.

Go to 76.

64

The creature – whatever it is – approaches fast in a whirl of skittering legs and claws. It fills the shaft and the Doctor's vision.

For a second he locks eyes with it. The creature's eyes are full of venomous hate. Its fangs are razor-sharp.

The Doctor thrusts one long arm straight out, aiming his sonic screwdriver at the creature. The device flares into vivid blue life, sending waves of modulated sonic energy directly into the snarling face of his attacker.

The creature squeals louder than the screwdriver. The strobing blue light fills the Doctor's vision. There is a loud clang, and suddenly he is falling.

The Doctor tries to grab hold of something to stop his fall, but he's tumbling head first and touches nothing. He realises that a section of the shaft has just opened up beneath him, possibly activated by the sonic screwdriver, and he's dropped right through.

He falls, hits something hard, bounces off something else, and then finds himself sliding in the pitch dark down a long, metallic slope. Eventually he plunges head first off a ledge and hits the ground with a bone-jarring thump.

The Doctor climbs stiffly to his feet on a concrete floor.

Go to 57.

65

The Doctor can't put Kate at risk. He has to run.

There's no time to cross the tracks – the train will hit him and kill him instantly, and the Doctor has no desire to foolishly throw his life away.

But the creature on his back doesn't know or understand that.

With a terrible tearing and sucking noise, it pulls itself free, becoming visible as it does so.

Kate gapes in astonishment as the Doctor falls to his knees. The alien, which looks like a huge black insect, detaches itself from the Doctor, trailing long strands of mucus, and scurries away on its many legs.

'Don't let it get away,' the Doctor gasps.

Kate drops into a crouch, aiming her pistol carefully and coolly. Her fingers gently squeeze the trigger and the automatic thunders once, twice.

The first shot kicks dust up from the ground, but the second hits the creature somewhere near the thorax. It skids to a halt in a tangle of rigid limbs.

Kate runs up, pistol held low, to check it's dead.

'Don't go near it,' warns the Doctor.

Go to 99.

66

'So we're looking for a dangerous alien life form in the basement of the research complex,' Anjli says.

'Are you thinking aloud or just providing a useful narrative?' grumbles the Doctor. It's good to have company, but with company comes responsibility. *A duty of care.*

He turns to Anjli. 'You should really go back. Up the antigravity shaft, right to the top of the base. Find somewhere secure. Preferably a large blue police box. If you see one of those, go inside. Wait for me there. Don't touch anything.'

A low growl is the only response.

'That didn't sound good,' whispers Anjli.

The Doctor peers into a dark corner of the basement room. 'It isn't. Look.'

Two eyes peer straight back at them from the shadows. They are swiftly joined by another pair of eyes. And another.

'How many of them are there?' Anjli whispers.

'Just the one.'

It emerges, slowly, from the darkness. A crouched, misshapen beast of a thing, covered with tar-black scales and spikes of blood-crusted hair. A wide, fang-filled hole opens with a horrible sucking noise beneath a fruit bowl of mad, staring eyes.

'It's all right,' says the Doctor softly. He holds out a hand, gently, cautiously, trying not to alarm the creature. 'We mean you no harm.'

The beast bares its hideous fangs, lips peeling back until the jaws distend and open wide to reveal a snakes' nest of tongues. Each tongue squirms and gropes from the mouth like an independent living thing struggling to get free.

'I have really, really seen more than I want to,' says Anjli unhappily.

'I told you to go back,' the Doctor replies, without taking his eyes off the monster for a second.

'I want to. But I'm too scared to go on my own.'

'You'll be fine. Now go.'

'But – but what about you, Doctor?'

'Me? I want to stay here and have a chat with my new friend. It probably just wants to talk . . .'

The tongues suddenly shoot out of the beast's gaping mouth and slither along the floor towards them, tips groping like blind fingers.

If you think Anjli should leave, go to 71.

If you think she should stay with the Doctor, go to 120.

67

Somewhere up above him, hiding in the shadows, is the malignocite. The creature has ascended to a metal platform where it waits, trapped, its many legs quivering beneath it. The Doctor climbs the metal stairway after it, the determined scrape of his boots echoing off every step.

He hesitates. If the thing jumps for him now, the impact will take them both off the stairway and they will plummet to their deaths. It's a hundred-metre drop.

The Doctor advances slowly. His baleful gaze never leaves the spitting, snarling mass at the end of the walkway.

'You're cornered,' the Doctor tells it. 'There's no way out – except down, and that's a one-way trip.'

'*You come to slaughter me,*' the creature hisses.

'No. I do not slaughter.'

'*Then what? Will you save me?*'

The Doctor considers this. 'Are you worth saving?'

'*Who are you to judge me – any more than I can judge you?*'

'You've been in my mind,' the Doctor says. 'You know me. I can save you.'

'*Yet my existence is an abnormality – a scientific experiment gone wrong. I have but one desire: to survive.*'

'Ah yes, but therein lies the rub, doesn't it?' The Doctor leans casually against the rail. 'To be or not to be. No? Perhaps you weren't in my mind long enough to absorb Shakespeare. Just the English language. It's for the best, I suppose. I don't think I could stand a theatrical mind-controlling malignocite as well as a philosophical one.'

'*There is nothing left for me, except destruction.*'

'Och, come on! Don't be such a Debbie Downer. There's always hope. You can change.'

'*I cannot change my nature, which is in itself unnatural.*'

'Wait!' the Doctor cries out but it is too late. The creature allows itself to fall, silently, and the Doctor can only watch as it grows smaller in his vision and then hits the ground with a hard, echoing crunch a hundred metres below.

He walks slowly back down the stairs with heavy hearts. The malignocite lies broken in a pool of congealing green blood; an unhappy end for an unhappy monster.

THE END

68

The Doctor veers towards the wide-open mouth of a shaft. It's the main exhaust vent for the research complex, where all the toxic gases are expelled into space.

Still holding the deep breath he took before jumping from the shuttle, the Doctor dives straight into the shaft. Down, down he drops . . .

He allows his body to reach a state of almost pure suspended animation to conserve what little oxygen remains. He can survive for longer than a human without breathing, but not indefinitely.

He disappears into the shadows, a tiny speck of light growing gradually dimmer.

He is aware of falling, as if in a dream. He remembers diving out of a castle window, into a sea full of skulls. His head swims with memories: the Veil, the Confession Dial, the wall of unbreakable Azbantium . . . the Doctor draws strength from the memory. If he survived all that, then surely he can survive this?

He reaches the bottom of the deep shaft and manages to land without breaking any bones.

He gets stiffly to his feet. There's no sign of Jiao or the other scientists. Presumably they have drifted off course during the descent. He hopes they manage to survive. He hopes *he* manages to survive . . .

Using his sonic screwdriver to open an access door in the base of the shaft, the Doctor enters the research-complex basement.

Go to 57.

As the Doctor begins to crawl away, he can feel the creature's lashing stings whipping the air over his head. The only thing the Doctor can do is try to draw the thing's attention away from Kate and the UNIT soldiers.

The first sting lands heavily on his back, ripping through the material of his jacket. The next three strike in exactly the same place, directed by the instinct of a natural predator.

The poison sinks deep into the wound, and the Doctor gasps in pain.

The creature crawls after him, tentacles thrashing around its head in a frenzy.

'What do you want?' the Doctor turns and demands as the thing draws level. 'Do you want to get away from this planet? Because if you stay a minute longer the soldiers will kill you. They'll find a way – they always do. It's what they're good at.'

'*You can take us both off this miserable world!*' says the creature.

'We need to get back to my TARDIS.'

'*This could be a trick. How do I know I can trust you?*'

'That's rich, coming from you. Stay here and die, or come with me. It's your choice.'

Go to 25.

70

'Keep back,' says the Doctor, motioning Jiao away. 'Further back. Well out of range.'

Jiao takes a couple of uncertain steps back. 'Out of range? What do you mean?'

'The nanites are multiplying – millions of machines, all working together, building more machines from the surrounding material.'

Jiao is horrified. 'Surrounding material? You mean the professor's body?'

'I do. Right down to cellular level. Deconstructed, rebuilt, repurposed. It's quite brilliant.'

'It's horrible.'

The Doctor purses his lips, considering this. 'Yes, I suppose it is . . .'

'Shouldn't you stand back as well?'

'No need. It appears the malignocites are designed to

operate on human flesh only. I'm not human.'

'Something of an advantage at a time like this, then.'

'Which you, being eminently human, do not share.'

Jiao's eyes widen as Professor Hendrick's corpse seems to stir, and the dead mouth opens to emit a cloud of black vapour. It condenses into a thick black fog that hovers over the workbench.

'I don't like the look of that,' says the Doctor, frowning.

'What is it?'

'As much as I admire your need to identify the threat, at this point it's more important that we run.' The Doctor grabs her hand. 'So run!'

Go to 53.

71

'That's me done,' Anjli declares, and turns to run as the dismembered tongues slither towards the Doctor.

He can't really blame her. He'd quite like to run himself. But somehow he can't. Curiosity keeps him rooted to the spot. Always the need to find out *why* and *what* and *how* . . .

He watches the tongues grope closer. He stays absolutely still. He can tell by the way they move that they are completely blind. They are hunting by sound, or movement. Definitely not by scent – as well as not having any eyes, they don't appear to have noses either.

He watches them creep past his feet and slither through a gap between the rear of the chamber and the wall. Once he is sure they've gone, he turns to say something to Anjli and then remembers that she has left him.

The tongue-snakes seem to be moving with a purpose. Moving carefully so as not to draw attention to himself, the

Doctor follows them through the narrow gap. He begins to wonder if Anjli might have had the right idea after all. Beyond is a dark passage with rough stone walls that press in from either side.

Ahead, he can see dim electric light. He emerges into another part of the basement . . .

Go to 57.

72

'Kate!'

The name echoes around the darkened shed.

The Doctor watches carefully, waiting for the last echoing call to die away.

Then, slowly, Kate walks out of the shadows.

She looks at the Doctor with dimmed eyes and then collapses, outstretched, on the ground.

The Doctor kneels in the dust by her body. Thankfully she is still alive, but she's unconscious.

The Doctor looks up as something crawls out of the darkness behind Kate. It is the creature.

'So you have relinquished your control of my friend,' the Doctor says stonily. 'A very good idea.'

'*She could not sustain me!*' the creature hisses. '*But you can . . . and you will!*'

'Been there, done that,' replies the Doctor. 'And I'm telling you now, it's not going to happen.'

'*All living things will eventually bow down to the malignocite!*'

The Doctor's eyes narrow dangerously. 'Malignocite? Don't make me laugh. I can think of much better names for you. Parasite. Aberration. Monster. Need I go on?'

'*You will talk your way to an early death, Doctor!*'

'I've been around for a very, very long time. Whenever I die, it will not be early. Your time, however, is almost certainly up.'

The creature hisses angrily. '*Kneel down before me!*'

Go to 105.

73

The Doctor and Penny free-fall from the top of the lab complex towards the surface of the moon.

'Bend your knees when you land!' shouts the Doctor.

Penny rolls as she hits the dusty surface. The Doctor lands like an expert gymnast next to her.

'How are we even alive?' Penny gasps.

'The gravity here is half that of Earth's,' replies the Doctor.

Penny looks back up at the distant viewing deck. 'That was insanely dangerous.'

'But not as insanely dangerous as staying up there with a lot of fire-damaged malignocites. They didn't look very happy.'

'There is one thing you've overlooked,' Penny says, struggling for breath now. 'This moon may have half Earth's gravity . . . but it also has only . . . a quarter of Earth's atmosphere.'

'I knew that,' replies the Doctor instantly. 'Which is why it's vital to get you back inside the base as soon as possible.'

'Is that . . . wise?' Penny's legs are getting weaker.

The Doctor helps her up. 'The less insanely dangerous option is often the best.'

He leads her to the nearest airlock and aims his sonic screwdriver.

'Does that thing work on anything?' Penny asks.

'Nearly anything,' the Doctor replies, frowning. He stops and fiddles with the screwdriver. 'Unless it's something made of wood – which this clearly isn't. Maybe it's deadlock-sealed.'

He tries the sonic again.

If you think the sonic will open the airlock, go to 118.

If you think the airlock will stay shut, go to 83.

74

Without hesitation, the Doctor dives head first into the vent. The malignocites try to follow, but they are too bulky to fit through the opening.

Angrily they tear at the narrow mouth of the exhaust vent, sending clanging echoes down its entire length. The Doctor rattles around in the tube as it reverberates with the creatures' furious roars.

Gradually the noise recedes into the distance.

At which point the Doctor finds himself stuck. In the dark. The vent tube has narrowed, and he's lodged upside-down. He can feel the blood rushing to his head.

He wriggles his shoulders and feet but there's no movement. Panic is only heartbeats away.

He forces himself to calm down, closing his eyes and breathing deeply.

Gradually, using a series of muscle contractions and

extensions, he manages to move slowly downward. 'At least gravity is on my side,' he reflects.

He climbs out of the vent into a bare underground room. He thinks he can hear noises in the distance. Human voices? Or malignocite growls?

If you think the Doctor should investigate the noises, go to 57.

If you think he should try to get away, go to 75.

75

Quietly, the Doctor turns to leave – but finds one of the creatures standing right behind him. Sharp pincers close painfully on his arms, cutting into the material of his jacket. 'Ouch! Be careful with those things. You'll cause an injury.'

The creature drags the Doctor into a labyrinth of caves veined with luminous minerals. The ghostly glow reveals a nightmare scene: cell after cell of human remains – skeletons, rotting corpses and some poor souls only recently deceased.

Each cell takes the form of a deep pit cut into the bedrock off the main passageway. The Doctor is thrown into one of the pits and left in a crumpled heap at the bottom.

'Good evening,' says a voice in the gloom.

The Doctor is surprised to find that he is sharing the cell with an elderly human scientist.

'I'm Professor Goode.' The old man smiles weakly. 'I'm very sorry, but you find me in rather reduced circumstances.'

'Think nothing of it, professor. I'm the Doctor. Very pleased to meet you.'

'I'm afraid it's a bit late for me, Doctor. My left leg is broken in at least two places and my right kneecap is smashed. It was the fall, you know, when those blighters – they're called malignocites, you know – threw me in here. Pity they didn't just drop me full on the old bean. A cracked skull might've solved all my problems.'

'I can see why escape hasn't been a priority for you.'

'Escape? To where? Those devils are running everything down here.'

'Tell me what happened.'

'We were experimenting on trace minerals found beneath the lunar surface. The biogenetic enzymes were ideal for combining into intelligent nanotechnology. I'm afraid it all got a bit out of hand . . .'

'Breeding will out, professor. The malignocite DNA appears to be very powerful. It will have overwritten anything you came up with for the nanites.'

'And then some. Those monsters killed most of the base personnel and dragged a few down here – as sacrifices for their abominable leader!'

If you think the Doctor should try to escape straight away, go to 91.

If you think he should find out more first, go to 115.

The Doctor runs blindly until, by pure luck, he stumbles across an ancient control room. It's furnished entirely in wood, like the study of a Victorian explorer, with a modest central console and a set of stairs leading up to the exit doors.

'Perfect!' he exclaims as the creatures pour into the room after him. He bounds up the steps and bursts through the doors, emerging from the familiar police-box shape of the TARDIS into a brightly lit laboratory. He looks around, then quickly dives for cover under a nearby workbench.

The creatures swarm through the lab and disappear through secondary exits and ventilation shafts. A minute later all is quiet in the lab and the Doctor slowly stands up from where he has been crouched.

Next to him, also standing up, is a young woman in the uniform of a scientist. Her name tag says ANJLI.

'Are you here to help?' she asks anxiously.

'If I can,' the Doctor admits, casting an uncertain glance after the last of the creatures.

'They're malignocites,' Anjli tells him. 'Beings made from nanomachines gone bad. We're all infected with them here.'

'All?'

'I'm one of the last survivors on the base. The malignocites got into everyone else's bloodstream. They develop for twenty-four hours and then bioengineer a bodily metamorphosis into those . . . things.'

'Yes, I've just been given quite a run-around by them. Fascinating creatures.' The Doctor follows Anjli through to a mortuary, where a number of bodies are laid out on tables. 'What happened here? Why haven't these people already turned into malignocite monsters?'

'They killed themselves rather than suffer the change. The nanites die along with the host body. Suicide is the only known preventative measure.'

'Well, we'll have to see if we can improve on that.' The Doctor leads Anjli out of the lab and down via an antigravity lift shaft through the levels of the base.

'What are you looking for?' Anjli asks, trying to keep up.

'Monsters,' comes the reply as they reach the basement. 'I have to find out exactly what I'm dealing with here.'

Go to 66.

77

'But we should at least try to communicate with it,'
insists the Doctor.

Kate shakes her head. 'It took over your mind and it could
have killed you. It tried to kill me.'

The Doctor grumbles something in reply. He's noticed that
the sting on Kate's face has almost disappeared.

'Fast-acting, high-intensity nerve toxin in the sting,' Kate
tells him. 'Decays quickly though. Hellishly painful but non-
lethal, so long as you don't get too many at once.'

The Doctor touches the wounds on his own face and neck.
'I thought I was going to regenerate,' he says.

'You always were a bit of a drama queen.'

'But if it's not actually lethal, do you have to kill it?'

'It's a hostile invader, Doctor. My orders are clear.'

The helicopter flies in a wide circle over the railyard,
checking that the creature is alone and the ground troops

have retreated to a safe distance.

'We're all clear,' she says. 'Cordon in place.'

She signals to the pilot of the helicopter and he gives her the thumbs up. The chopper dips, circling the creature below. Then a series of rockets fire from the stubby wings beneath the fuselage and streak towards the ground.

There's a massive, brilliant blast of energy. The helicopter is buffeted by the shockwaves, and dust and debris fly high into the air in a great cloud of destruction.

The Doctor watches sadly as the smoke clears to reveal a shallow crater. There is nothing left of the alien.

When the helicopter lands, the Doctor is first out, running low to the ground beneath the rotors. Kate joins him by the crater.

'I don't even know what it was,' the Doctor complains.

'Hostile,' says Kate.

'Perhaps it was only doing what comes naturally,' argues the Doctor. 'Like a tiger is hostile.'

'Perhaps. But we still couldn't let it run free, endangering innocent people. Could we?'

The Doctor doesn't reply. He has no answer.

'Sometimes, things just work out wrong no matter what you do,' Kate tells him gently.

THE END

78

The Doctor cringes in agony as the Malignocite Prime tightens its telepathic grip.

'*Animal scum,*' snarls the monster.

'What is an UnderGod anyway?' The Doctor forces himself to look up through bloodshot eyes. 'And what's the Lower Dark, while we're at it?'

'*Bah!*' The Malignocite Prime directs a wave of telepathic rage through the Doctor's brain. '*I could crush you in an instant, Time Lord!*'

'That temper is going to be a problem. Wait – what do you know about the Time Lords?'

'*The Time Lords drove me out of the Old Universe. They thought I was dead. But I have waited in the Lower Dark for millennia. I have grown more powerful – I lured you to this barren world, Doc-tor. I sensed your time ship in the Vortex!*'

The Doctor frowns. 'Then you are indeed very powerful.'

'*Kneel before my telepathic might, Doc-tor!*'

'I would prefer to stand – all this kneeling is wearing holes in my trousers.' The Doctor climbs unsteadily to his feet. 'You won't crush me – not if you want my TARDIS.'

'*You have no choice. The TARDIS is mine!*'

A shimmering cone of light appears on the altar, and the TARDIS materialises.

Go to 97.

79

An old man in white overalls shuffles into the storeroom. He looks at the Doctor in complete surprise.

'Good grief! Who the devil are you?'

'The Doctor. Now I have a question for you: What in the name of all space and time is going on here?'

The old man blinks uncertainly. 'My name is Professor Hardacre.'

'I don't remember asking who you are. I distinctly remember asking what's going on here, though.' The Doctor points a long finger at the old spacesuits. 'And I think I should warn you I've had a very long day.'

'Well, erm, Doctor . . . I was part of a scientific elite researching biogenetic nanotechnology, and –'

'Was?' The Doctor's eyes narrow. He doesn't like elites.

'Yes. I have renounced my involvement. Why, I couldn't be part of what they wanted to do.'

'Why? What did they want you to do?'

'We were working on a project to create bio-weapons.'
Professor Hardacre sits down with a weary sigh. 'But the
truth was kept from most of the research staff, who were kept
focused on specific areas of the project so that no one could
see the "whole picture". I realised the truth, however, and
resigned my post just before it all went disastrously wrong.'

'What's happened to all the others?' demands the Doctor.
'Or are you the only one with a conscience?'

Go to 109.

80

There's no time to waste. The Doctor sprints after Kate, his long legs pumping hard. She crosses the railway tracks and the Doctor hurtles after her, being careful to check there are no more trains approaching. That would be an undignified way to go, after all.

He chases Kate across the scrubland separating the tracks. Long grass and weeds, made brittle by the season, lash at his shins. He is soon panting hard. The ordeal with the creature has left him more drained than he had thought.

Kate is getting away – or rather the creature controlling her is. The Doctor sees Kate stumble, perhaps exhausted, and the creature yanks her upright under its cruel mental lashing.

The Doctor cannot abide cruelty in any form. He vows to save Kate's life, even at the expense of the creature's.

Kate disappears into the dark entrance of an abandoned railway shed.

The Doctor follows her inside. It's dark and cold and echoing. The Doctor comes to a halt as the emptiness of the shed silently mocks him.

The creature has taken Kate into the shadows somewhere, out of sight.

If you think the Doctor should try to search for Kate, go to 90.

If you think he should call her to come out of hiding instead, go to 72.

81

'*You will open the TARDIS for me!*' cries the Malignocite Prime.

The Doctor looks up at the looming monster. 'Never willingly. You will have to make me.'

The Malignocite Prime's eyes bulge menacingly and the creature exerts its massive telepathic will. The Doctor feels the monster taking over his mind. His hand, no longer under his own control, extends towards the TARDIS and inserts the key. His fingers turn the key. The police box door opens . . . And the Doctor dashes inside, slamming it shut behind him.

He races to the control console and activates the scanner screen. The seething fury of the Malignocite Prime fades into view.

'You made a mistake trusting me, you know,' the Doctor says. He operates the controls and the TARDIS growls into life. 'Your telepathic control won't work in here – separate relative dimensions and all that. You're powerless now.'

The monster's voice echoes through the loudspeaker.

'*What . . . what are you doing?*'

'Something I don't often get the chance to do!'

The TARDIS dematerialises and the Malignocite Prime fades from view.

'I'm going back along my own timeline.' The Doctor smiles and winks. 'I'm going back to the beginning. And this time – things will be different!'

THE END

82

A group of UNIT soldiers arrives with a tarpaulin to cover the dead creature.

'Make sure you call in the rest of the clean-up squad,' orders Kate. 'Fusion cremation at the Stonehenge facility followed by a full decontamination sweep of this entire area.'

'What about the Doctor, ma'am?' asks the sergeant.

'Leave him to me.'

Kate nudges the Doctor with her toe. 'I haven't got time for layabouts in UNIT, Doctor.'

The Doctor opens one eye. 'I'm not in UNIT.'

'Exactly.'

The Doctor groans. 'Kate, I'm dying . . .'

'Well, here's something that might make you feel better.'

A UNIT lorry rumbles to a halt nearby, and a couple of squaddies pull back the cover to reveal an old blue police box sitting on the flatbed.

'The TARDIS!' The Doctor, energised, climbs unsteadily to his feet.

Kate helps him over to the lorry as a forklift truck lowers the police box to the ground. 'I thought the sight of this old thing might do the trick.'

Hands trembling, the Doctor unlocks the TARDIS and pushes open the door. The light spills out and bathes his gaunt features. He sighs. 'That's better!'

'So you're not regenerating then?'

'The TARDIS has certain restorative properties for a Time Lord.'

'Well, don't let me get in your way.' Kate smiles, stepping back.

The Doctor hesitates. 'Just one thing. The alien, whatever it was – I'm sorry it had to end like that.'

'It tricked you, Doctor. It was a good job I was here.

Sometimes there has to be someone willing to pull a trigger.'

'It's a point of view,' the Doctor concedes. 'But not one I'm happy to share.'

He steps into the TARDIS, and closes the door, then opens it immediately and looks back out. 'One more thing.'

'Yes?'

'Why don't you come with me?'

Kate smiles again. 'With my gun, you mean? I don't think so, Doctor. It wouldn't work out.'

He nods sadly. 'No, I don't suppose it would. Worth a try, though.'

And, with that, he closes the door of the TARDIS and is gone.

THE END

83

The airlock refuses to open.

'Deadlock-sealed!' exclaims the Doctor with annoyance.

'What now?' Penny asks.

The Doctor looks back up and points. 'Dinner – with us on the menu.'

The malignocites have followed them out of the viewing dome. Some are crawling down the vertical sides of the base tower. Some are floating down through the half gravity.

'Run!' Penny yells.

They head towards the outer sections of the lab complex. But they are soon running short of breath in the moon's thin atmosphere. The malignocites don't seem to be affected. They swarm over the surface of the moon after them. The leader – the largest – is still trailing smoke.

The Doctor and Penny skid to a halt in a cloud of dust. They've reached some kind of exhaust port shaped like a funnel.

'Gas vent,' Penny explains quickly. 'Leads to the basement.'

'What about that?' The Doctor points at a black opening in the moon rock – the entrance to a cave.

'Leads to the catacombs beneath the base,' says Penny.

'Let's split up,' says the Doctor. 'You take one, I'll take the other.'

If you think the Doctor should take the gas vent, go to 74.

If you think he should head into the cave, go to 34.

84

The Doctor lets Jiao lead him through the outer sections of the lab complex until they reach the shuttle. Looking out through a porthole, they can see the stubby, rocket-shaped vessel standing on the launch pad. Wisps of steam drift from the thrusters and float away in a cloud of sparkling ice particles in the vacuum.

'Good,' says Jiao. 'They've already got the engines running. We can take off straight away.'

The Doctor is peering back down the corridor. He can hear the angry buzz of the nanite cloud not far behind.

'It's gaining on us,' Jiao notes.

The Doctor nods grimly. 'It's working out how to get through the airlocks faster every time. The whole cloud is one big, artificial intelligence. Give it a bit longer and it'll be the cleverest thing for light years. Apart from me, of course.'

'Come on!'

Jiao leads him through the last airlock, punching the security-code sequence with urgent stabs of her finger. The door sighs open and they run through as the cloud hisses behind them.

There's no time to lock it. They sprint down the access corridor and arrive at the shuttle's boarding hatch.

The cloud swarms behind them.

Go to 116.

85

The creature nests in a swarm of wriggling pupae. It sits on a swollen gut of translucent skin through which more of the squirming chrysalises can be seen.

Rising above the grotesque orb of its lower body is a hunched torso from which distorted limbs emerge between joints in the hard outer shell. The limbs are useless for movement; they are merely reminders of whatever means of propulsion the beast once knew. They quiver and jerk spasmodically, ungoverned by conscious thought, located beneath an extended jaw that is continuously open and drooling a brackish slime.

But by far the worst aspect of the creature is its eyes, which are plentiful, bulging from its skull like diseased pustules, some blind and leaking, others distended and madly rolling, but all filled with devilish spite.

Grimly the Doctor realises that it is from this malignant

form that all the others have been produced, either naturally in this underground incubator, or artificially in the laboratories above.

Hidden behind a stalagmite, the Doctor considers his next move.

If you think the Doctor should get closer, go to 117.

If you think he should withdraw before he's seen, go to 75.

86

'I can help you,' says the Doctor.

The creature hisses, full of suspicion. '*Explain!*'

'I can take you back to the world you came from.' The Doctor knows that time is running short; the alien poison is taking its toll on his body. 'And you can help me find an antidote to your sting.'

'*Impossible!*'

'We have to try. Otherwise these soldiers will kill you. You're already wounded, and so am I. Neither of us belongs on this world.' The Doctor looks into the creature's many pain-filled eyes. 'We should leave.'

Kate draws her automatic pistol. 'He means it,' she tells the creature. 'And so do I.'

The wound on her face is already healing, but the Doctor has suffered far greater injuries. He knows he doesn't have long left.

'*Very well,*' snarls the creature. '*Take me to your conveyance.*'

The Doctor closes his eyes in relief. 'On one condition: you let me drive. You're a passenger only.'

Kate organises a group of UNIT squaddies to fetch the TARDIS on a flatbed lorry. The old police box is lowered to the ground and the Doctor unlocks the door with trembling fingers.

'Inside,' he tells the creature. 'Now.'

Go to 25.

87

The Doctor explodes out of the cupboard and launches himself at the person with the gun.

They go down in a tangle of arms and legs. The gun goes off: a laser blast which digs chunks of concrete out of the ceiling, showering them both in dust.

The Doctor grabs the wrist of the hand holding the laser and pushes it down against the floor. The figure wriggles underneath him but releases the gun. Distracted for a second by the clatter, the Doctor is thrown clear and his opponent jumps to their feet.

'Stay away from me, you alien freak!'

The Doctor looks up to see a young woman with red hair standing over him. 'Oi! Less of the "freak"!'

The woman stoops to pick up her laser but the Doctor gets there first. He stands up, levelling the pistol at her. 'Let's try the introductions again,' he says.

'My name is Kala. And you attacked me, you alien freak!'

'Try again,' the Doctor says, charging the laser.

Kala eyes the pistol, aware that a single blast would now burn a hole straight through her heart. 'My name is Kala. But you attacked me, Mr . . .?'

'Doctor.'

If you think the Doctor should give the gun back, go to 93.

If you think he should keep the gun, go to 88.

88

'Give me back my gun,' says Kala, holding out her hand. 'Hurry! I don't have time for this.'

'Manners,' says the Doctor warningly. 'Try again.'

'Give me back my gun, *please*.'

'That's better. But I'll keep the gun for now, thanks. I love guns, me. *Pew! Pew!*' The Doctor pretends to shoot targets around the room. Then he straightens up and looks at the laser with contempt. 'Actually, I hate guns. I always think they make me look a bit silly. A bit *pathetic*. Here, you have it.'

He tosses the pistol across the room and Kala catches it, surprised. She looks back at the Doctor, who raises an eyebrow and smiles.

'Now we've got past introductions and guns and all that boring stuff,' he says, 'let's talk about monsters.'

'You've seen the malignocites?'

'A little too much of them. A little too many dead people, too.'

'They've run riot throughout the base. There's hardly

anyone left alive. We've set the base to self-destruct. I'm going to escape with the others in the space shuttle – and there's not much time left. I'll shoot my way there if I have to!'

'It may be a little late for that,' warns the Doctor.

Kala shakes her head. 'One shuttle's already left. I was heading for the other shuttle. Come on!'

Go to 95.

89

The Doctor pulls the locker door closed very, very carefully.

He listens, still not daring to breathe, as the footsteps come closer. *Whoever it is has a gun, and guns seldom mean anything good,* the Doctor reflects. Trapped in this locker, he's a sitting duck. He can only hope the person moves on as soon as possible. They sound like they're in a hurry.

Seconds stretch as the footsteps come closer.

The Doctor tries to shrink back among the brooms and mops. He's thin, but he doubts even he can be mistaken for a broom handle.

The footsteps draw closer.

Suddenly the locker door is pulled open and the Doctor is staring down the barrel of a fully charged laser pistol.

'You won't find that very useful,' he tells the owner. 'If you shoot me, you'll never survive on the base. And if you don't shoot me – well, what's the point of having it?'

The owner is a young woman in red security overalls with a name badge that says KALA.

'What the hell are you doing in here?'

'Hiding,' the Doctor says. 'Rather obvious, isn't it?'

'I mean, what are you still doing down here in the basement? Everyone else has been evacuated on the space shuttles. If we're quick, we may still get to the last one!'

The Doctor steps out of the locker and dusts himself down. 'Do we really have to talk at gunpoint?'

'It's for self-defence,' Kala tells him curtly. 'Get moving.'

'What's the hurry?'

'In case you hadn't noticed, this entire base is crawling with malignocites.'

'I had noticed,' the Doctor assures her, 'and I was rather hoping to do something about it.'

'It's too late. The base has been set to self-destruct. We need to leave right now.'

The Doctor follows Kala out of the basement and into a storeroom. From there they head for the antigravity shafts leading to the research-base level.

Go to 95.

90

The Doctor puts on his sonic sunglasses and scans the railway shed. For a few seconds all that can be heard is the shrill whine of the infrared lenses echoing through the darkness.

Then he sees Kate.

She's curled up beneath a set of metal steps leading to a higher level. She's hiding like a child, her eyes tightly shut. Her breathing is very shallow. The alien has drained her of all energy.

The Doctor crouches down. 'Kate? It's the Doctor. It's going to be all right.'

Her eyes open and something evil glares through them at the Doctor.

'*Come any closer and I'll eat your throat!*' The voice is harsh, gurgling – an alien's attempt to manipulate a human throat into making words.

'Really?' says the Doctor. 'I'd like to see you try, malignocite.

Yes, that's what I'm going to call you. That's what's going to be written on your grave.'

Kate's energy is spent and the creature knows it. With an angry squeal it becomes visible and scuttles off her back, heading for the metal steps.

The Doctor quickly checks that Kate is unharmed, then sets off in pursuit of the alien.

Go to 67.

91

'As much as I like a good chat – and I actually don't – I'm afraid I'm going to have to leave you,' says the Doctor.

Professor Goode nods sadly. 'I understand. There's nothing you can do for me here, Doctor.'

'I can do something, and I will. But first I need help. And for that I've got to get out of here.'

The professor smiles. 'I'm afraid giving you a leg up is out of the question.'

'Don't worry, I'll manage.' Using a series of tiny hollows and depressions in the rock, the Doctor scrambles awkwardly out of the pit.

'Godspeed!' calls the professor.

But the Doctor has already gone. Moving silently through the caves, dodging malignocite patrols, he tries to find a way to the exit.

'I think I may have taken a wrong turn,' he whispers.

Squeezing through a narrow crevice in the cave wall, the Doctor has emerged behind a raised platform carved from solid rock. On top of the platform is the first of the malignocites – a giant beast bristling with useless limbs and eyes filled with red-rimmed madness.

The Doctor can hear the sounds of malignocite guards behind him. He can't go back.

Go to 117.

92

With an impatient snarl, the Malignocite Prime snatches the key from the Doctor's hand. Then, using one of its more dexterous limbs, the monster inserts the key into the police box lock.

There is an instant of complete silence, as if a connection is being made with something deep and terrible in the universe.

The Malignocite Prime is frozen, its eyes bulging in horror.

'I don't suppose this is what you were expecting,' the Doctor says calmly.

'*What . . . is . . . happening?*'

'You are an old and ancient enemy of the Time Lords. They take that kind of thing very seriously. They make every TARDIS into a trap for the likes of you.'

The Malignocite Prime seethes, but it cannot let go of the key.

'As soon as the TARDIS sensed your biogenetic presence through the key, it started an ancient Time Lord protocol deep within its time matrix. Right now, the TARDIS is tracking back along your timeline, unpicking you from the fabric of the universe.'

'*Not . . . possible!*'

'Minute by minute, second by second, you're being disconnected from time.' The Doctor watches as the Malignocite Prime turns slowly transparent. 'Everything you've done here, every part of you, is being removed from the universe.'

'*You must . . . stop . . . it!*'

'I wish I could – if I thought there was a way, or there was any hope for you.' The Doctor's eyes turn cold and blue beneath the frowning brows. 'Unfortunately, there is neither.'

'*This is an . . . execution!*'

The Doctor winces. The Malignocite Prime's voice is now barely audible, its body barely visible.

'It is a trap that has waited millennia to be sprung.'

And then the Malignocite Prime is gone – vanished from the universe forever.

After a moment's hesitation, the Doctor turns the key in the TARDIS lock and steps inside.

THE END

93

The Doctor hands the laser pistol back to Kala. 'Not really my style, is it?'

Kala eyes him dubiously. 'Sensor readings said there was an alien in the basement.'

'Well, I am an alien, but it's not me you should be shooting. Are you looking for the alien biogenetic data stored in the nanites?'

'You know what's going on here?'

'Enough to tell you to get off the base as soon as possible.'

'I'm heading for the shuttle transporter,' Kala says. 'If we're careful and we can avoid the malignocites, we might make it.'

'You can go,' the Doctor tells her. 'I'm staying. I need to find the source of the alien biogenetic data.'

'It was extracted from beneath the moon's surface,' Kala says. 'There are caves running under the lab complex.'

At the Doctor's insistence, Kala leads him deeper into the

basement storerooms until they reach a flight of stone steps that lead down into the caves.

'Leave me here,' he tells her. 'Get back to the transporter, and get out of here with everyone else you can find.'

Kala hesitates and then offers him the laser. 'Why don't you take this?'

'No thanks.' He frowns. 'Like I said – not really my style.'

Go to 34.

94

Before he can warn anyone, the creature digs into the Doctor's mind and forces him to turn sharply away from Kate. The sudden movement spooks the soldiers and one of them opens fire.

The bullet hits the creature. The Doctor feels the impact and the creature squeals in pain, suddenly becoming visible.

Kate recoils in horror as a dark, pus-like slime oozes from the bullet hole.

And then a long, lashing tentacle emerges from the wound, flailing like a whip.

The tip strikes Kate across the cheek and she cries out, falling to the ground.

Shocked, the rest of Grey Division opens fire. Round after round finds its mark on the creature's hard, shell-like back. The Doctor staggers to his knees as the creature falls off him, shuddering and squirming under the onslaught.

Slime bubbles from its wounds.

'You stupid fools!' the Doctor gasps. 'Will you never learn?'

The creature lets out a blood-curdling shriek and fresh tentacles erupt from the bullet holes and whip around in a frenzy.

If you think the Doctor should get a safe distance away, go to 69.

If you think he should stop to help Kate instead, go to 100.

95

Kala leads the Doctor along the corridors to an antigravity shaft.

'Wait,' says the Doctor. 'Did you say the base was set to self-destruct?'

'Yes,' Kala replies. 'Come on!'

The Doctor quickly follows Kala up the antigravity shaft. 'How long have we got?'

'Less than four minutes, now – so hurry up.'

The Doctor pulls Kala to a halt as they emerge from the shaft. 'We'll never make it to the shuttle launch pad. It's too far, and there are too many malignocites in the way. I've got a better idea!'

He turns back and heads through the laboratory complex. Kala follows him, protesting all the way. 'Your idea better be good!'

'My idea involves an old blue police box and relative

dimensions. It's better than good – and you get to survive.'

The Doctor uses his sonic screwdriver to open a door but Kala gasps in dismay. Beyond is a laboratory full of corpses strewn across the floor. All of them appear to have been skinned alive.

'The malignocites have been here,' she says.

'They dismantle the molecular structure from the outside in, using aggressive nanotechnology,' the Doctor confirms, checking the nearest body using the sonic. 'I wonder why they're storing the remains in here?'

'We now have less than two minutes before we die in a gigantic explosion,' Kala interrupts. 'Just saying.'

'The TARDIS is just through here,' the Doctor tells her. 'Big blue box. You can't miss it.'

They step over the corpses, and make their way across the laboratory. When they reach the far end, the Doctor opens the door . . . to reveal a snarling malignocite.

It smashes the Doctor to the ground with a ferocious blow, opening its sharp jaws to encompass his head. The Doctor aims his sonic screwdriver, but it has no effect; the monster bends down, ready to decapitate him.

A series of laser blasts drive the creature backwards, blowing chunks out of its armoured hide.

Kala pulls the Doctor up, still brandishing the laser.

'All right, *sometimes* it's useful,' he admits.

'Thirty seconds!' yells Kala.

The Doctor pushes her into the old blue police box. 'In here!'

The TARDIS door slams shut, the grinding roar of its engines disappearing in the noise of an explosion which destroys the entire research base and half the moon.

THE END

The TARDIS materialises in the centre of the darkened main laboratory. A thin haze of dust swirls around the police box as the door snaps open and the Doctor steps out.

The creature follows him. Both move slowly, weak and near death.

'Where's the antidote?' asks the Doctor. 'You said there would be an antidote for the toxins you put into my bloodstream.'

Ignoring him, the creature creeps across the laboratory. It doesn't seem so weak now.

'You've perked up,' remarks the Doctor suspiciously.

'*My body can cope with impact wounds, given sufficient time to recover.*'

'Well, lucky you.' The Doctor is frowning. He doesn't like the way this is turning out at all.

The creature uses its mandibles to open a hatch in the lab

wall, and begins to crawl inside.

'Wait,' says the Doctor. 'What about my antidote?'

'*Fend for yourself, Time Lord!*'

And, with that, the creature climbs into the hatch and disappears.

The Doctor stumbles across the room and looks through the hatch. Some kind of access tunnel or shaft.

'Come back!' His voice echoes with pitiful anger.

The Doctor sits down in shock. Abandoned! Betrayed! Of all the cheek.

Go to 128.

97

The Doctor watches in mute fascination as his TARDIS materialises on the altar.

'That's a good trick,' he admits. 'How's it done? Mirrors? Trap door?'

'*Your prattling is merely an attempt to hide your fear, Doc-tor,*' says the Malignocite Prime. '*Pitiful in its way.*'

The Doctor climbs on to the altar and touches the TARDIS. 'Not an illusion,' he mutters, disappointed. Suddenly he clicks his fingers and points at the Malignocite Prime. 'Got it! Telekinetic matter transportation! Oh, that's good. Very good. Very powerful.'

'*Enough,*' snarls the Malignocite Prime. '*Open the TARDIS!*'

'You can't make me do that.'

'*I can and I will!*'

'I mean – you've beaten me already. I know you can force me to do it telepathically.' The Doctor looks down at his feet. 'But spare me that final humiliation, please.'

'*I will humiliate all the Time Lords! I will use your TARDIS to return to Gallifrey and lay waste to that miserable civilisation!*'

'I can't stop you,' the Doctor admits. 'Just don't make me open the TARDIS.'

'*Open the TARDIS for me, Doc-tor!*'

The Malignocite Prime looms over the Doctor. The TARDIS stands on the altar, its quiet hum a promise of massive, distant power just waiting to be unleashed.

Head bowed, the Doctor holds the TARDIS key out to the monster. 'Please. You mustn't make me do it.'

If you think the Malignocite Prime will force the Doctor to do it, go to 81.

If you think the creature will open the TARDIS itself, go to 92.

98

'Let me help you,' says the Doctor. 'And then you can help me.'

The creature hisses and writhes, full of suspicion. '*Explain!*'

'Let me take you back home – to the world you came from. Perhaps I can help you there.' The Doctor knows that time is running short; the alien poison is taking its toll on his body. 'And perhaps I can find an antidote to your sting.'

'*There is no antidote,*' the creature tells him. '*I am talking to a dead thing.*'

'I refuse to believe that! Just come with me to my TARDIS. I can analyse the toxin.'

'*Very well,*' the creature snarls. '*Come closer.*'

Nearly at the point of collapse, the Doctor automatically takes a step forward.

And the creature strikes.

Tentacles lash out and grip the Doctor's arms and legs.

'It's a trap!' screams Kate, running up behind the Doctor.

She aims her automatic and shoots round after round into the creature's head. The alien crumples, its long skull smashed to a pulp.

The quivering tentacles fall away from the Doctor, and he collapses. He has been stung again. The dose is lethal.

Go to 82.

99

'It's dead,' announces Kate, touching the creature with the toe of her boot. 'Thankfully.'

'When did you get so bloodthirsty?' wonders the Doctor as he climbs to his feet.

'When did you get so careless?' Kate turns on him angrily. 'Bringing that thing to Earth! Think of the consequences!'

'I'm always thinking of the consequences,' snaps the Doctor. 'I'm a Time Lord. My life is nothing *but* consequences.' He brushes dust from his jacket and hair, then sighs. 'The truth is . . . I had no choice. The creature was controlling me. It's an insanely powerful telekinetic life form.'

'And a parasite?'

'It used my brain like a battery. It would drain a human being in less than an hour.'

'And then?'

'Move on to the next one, and the next one after that.

Growing bigger and more powerful every time, until it doesn't even need to physically attach itself any more. It can do it all by remote control.'

'Then, like I said, good job it's dead.' Kate pokes the thing with her toe again, and it suddenly jerks into life, scrambling up her leg and attaching itself to her neck.

Go to 110.

The Doctor ducks beneath the flailing tentacles and crawls across the ground towards Kate.

The soldiers are reluctant to fire again on the creature. It's lying in the dirt, lashing madly around with a forest of long, black tentacles. Each one seems to be tipped with an evil-looking barb.

Kate is in a bad way. The wound on her face, where the first tentacle struck, is inflamed. She's still breathing, but she's unconscious. The Doctor tries to pull her out of the way of any more stings. Enough of them and they will surely be lethal.

But he's underestimated the savage fury of the alien. A series of stings lashes across the Doctor's back, shredding the material of his jacket. Several cut his face.

The pain is agonising but, free of the creature's mental control, the Doctor feels better able to deal with it. His priority is saving Kate. With supreme effort, he drags her far enough away to wait until a squad of UNIT troopers can carry her to safety.

The Doctor is left on his hands and knees. The stings on his face and neck are burning and his vision blurs.

Go to 17.

101

The Doctor races back to the TARDIS. His legs work hard to get him back up the hill to the place where it landed. He flings open the door and hurries to the controls, throwing the dematerialisation levers as he skids to a halt.

There's only one way the Doctor can think of to track Kate now: by finding the creature.

'You may have control of Kate's mind, but you had control of mine before that. You tasted Time Lord! And guess what?' the Doctor says, plunging his fingers into the soft telepathic circuits of the TARDIS control board. 'The Time Lord got a taste of you, too. I've still got that taste now, deep inside my mind. And if I can still get it, then so can my TARDIS!'

The rotors whirr and the central column shines brightly. The time machine shifts sideways through time and space and the engines roar in protest.

'Come on, I know you can do it!' the Doctor implores his

old ship. 'Do it. Just for me!'

With a resounding thud the TARDIS materialises around the alien being – and around Kate Stewart. The sudden change in dimensions disorientates both her and the creature, and she collapses to the floor.

The Doctor kicks the creature aside as it becomes visible and Kate groans with relief.

'I'd apologise,' the Doctor tells her, 'but it was the only way I could weaken it. Unfortunately, it's had the same effect on you.'

Before the creature can recover, the Doctor scoops Kate up and carries her out of the TARDIS. 'Not very dignified, but at least it gets you out of harm's way.'

He lays her gently on the ground outside and quickly locates her mobile phone. It's standard UNIT issue. A quick glance through the sonic glasses gives him full access and he dials Osgood's priority contact number. He puts the phone in

Kate's hand as she comes to, and then disappears back into the TARDIS. The Doctor staggers back to the console and flings the dematerialisation lever over once more.

The police box fades away before Kate's fully conscious.

Go to 56.

102

The Doctor activates the Time Vector Generator without hesitation. The device slips into his hand – it's like a short, black rod – and he dives out of the TARDIS just in time. There's a good reason why the Time Vector Generator is located next to the doors.

The inside of the TARDIS convulses and collapses until the inside is no bigger than the outside; it becomes little more than a police box.

The creatures hurtle out of the box in a sudden, panicked rush. They flap madly around the lab, screeching and scratching as they look for an exit.

The Doctor pockets the Time Vector Generator. It will be a disaster if he loses it – he needs it to restore the TARDIS to its proper dimensions.

The creatures swarm around the lab in confusion, but it won't be long before they find the Doctor.

He starts to crawl across the floor on his hands and knees, but one of the monsters appears in front of him. It's vaguely insectoid, with long, slavering jaws and many multijointed arms.

The Doctor fixes it with a hard stare. The creature stares back through a profusion of tiny, glittering black eyes.

"'And if thou gaze long into an abyss, the abyss will also gaze into thee",' the Doctor mutters. 'I think I'm beginning to understand what Nietzsche meant.'

The Doctor pulls out his sonic screwdriver and activates it on a low setting. He doesn't want to alarm the creature unduly. He waves the sonic gently to and fro until the monster seems to be completely subdued.

Then he inches his way slowly behind the nearest workbench and quietly gets to his feet. He's still holding his breath.

The creature turns and crawls away, climbing into a low vent in the wall.

'I wonder where you're off to?' Overcome with curiosity, the Doctor is about to follow, until he realises that there is a human body lying on the workbench in front of him.

If you think the Doctor should stop and examine the body, go to 19.

If you think he should follow the creature into the vent, go to 21.

103

Jiao nods, her lips tight. 'I guessed as much. What about you?'

'The malignocites have developed a taste for human DNA. I'm not human,' says the Doctor.

'So what do we do now?'

The Doctor aims his sonic screwdriver at a nearby computer console and calls up a map of the base. 'We have to get you off the moonbase before the nanites decide to come after us in numbers.'

Jiao points to the airlock at the rear of the lab. 'I think it may already be too late.'

'It's never too late,' the Doctor snaps, examining the map in careful detail. 'Corridor junction here, secondary lab complex here . . . aha. Emergency shuttle. I thought there would be one.'

'Doctor,' says Jiao urgently. 'It's the nanites!'

The Doctor looks up sharply as a black mist starts to drift

through the airlock into the lab.

'Get back against the far wall,' the Doctor orders quietly. 'It'll go for you first – you're the human.'

The cloud of nanites is starting to hum like a distant swarm of bees.

'Can you get us to the shuttle?' the Doctor asks.

'If we go through the outer labs, we may be able to make it.'

'Then what are we waiting for? Lead on, Jiao!'

Go to 84.

104

The Doctor steps into the antigravity shaft and activates it with his sonic screwdriver. He drops quickly down the narrow tube, level after level, until he feels his ears beginning to pop as the atmospheric pressure changes. The antigravity rays intensify as he reaches the bottom of the shaft and he slows to a halt.

'Ground floor: perfumery, stationery and leather goods.' The Doctor steps out of the lift shaft, straightening his cuffs.

'Now which way, Doctor?' he asks himself, peering along the gloomy corridor. 'I seem to have come rather a long way down.' He licks a finger and holds it up, testing the air. 'At least half a mile.' He smiles sadly, remembering that there is no one to show off to any more.

'Why are you doing that?' asks a voice. 'Licking your finger and holding it up.'

'I'm showing off,' the Doctor confesses, turning. 'And not

very well. Who are you?'

'Anjli. I'm a service engineer. What's going on? Where is everyone? Who are you?'

'I'm not sure, probably dead, and the Doctor. In that order.'

Anjli is dressed in blue overalls and work boots. There is a smudge of soot on her nose. 'Dead?' she repeats.

'There's an alien life form roaming the base,' the Doctor explains. His voice is terse, factual. 'If I had to classify it, I would say it's hostile.'

He heads deeper into the basement, and Anjli follows. 'Where are we going?' she asks.

'I was hoping you'd tell me that – you're the service engineer.'

'This way leads to the generators and life support. We're about as deep as you can go. Apart from the caves.'

'Caves?'

'The moon rock is like a honeycomb beneath the base.'

The Doctor frowns. 'Could the alien be indigenous to this moon? Perhaps the base has encroached on its territory. It may just be trying to defend itself.'

'I've no idea. What are you intending to do?'

'Find out.'

'Down here?'

'I've been following it and it's running scared – from me. I'm not popular with monsters.'

Go to 66.

'Kneel down?' The Doctor scoffs. 'Don't be ridiculous. For one thing, it would ruin my trousers. For another, I don't kneel down before anyone. Or anything.'

The creature hisses. It can no longer hide. It crawls into the light and glares with fiery, throbbing eyes.

'I knew you wouldn't last it out,' the Doctor says. His voice is withering but exhausted.

'*You have the means to escape this world, Doctor,*' says the creature. '*Take me with you and there will be no more casualties.*'

'Very well. But it has to be on my terms, in my TARDIS.'

Carefully, cautiously, aware that at any moment he could be caught in the crosshairs of a UNIT sniper rifle, the Doctor leads the creature back to the TARDIS.

'*A miraculous vessel, Doctor.*'

The police box stands exactly where it landed. The Doctor unlocks the door and ushers the beast through.

Inside, the Doctor sets the controls and the TARDIS dematerialises.

'*Where are you taking us?*' the creature demands.

'Back to where you belong.'

If you think the Doctor is tricking the creature, go to 56.

If you think the offer is genuine, go to 96.

106

The Doctor follows the sound deeper into the caves. The passageway grows narrower, with sheer rock walls pressing in on his shoulders until he's forced to turn sideways. He inches his way forward. Cobwebs envelop his face and he feels the spiders scuttling away as he breaks through the sticky strands.

The noise of the chanting grows ever louder. Ahead, he can see a flickering glow.

Eventually the Doctor emerges into a wide cavern lit by flaming torches. Immense stalagmites reach up to a soot-darkened ceiling.

Around the base of the craggy spires is a seething mass of insect life – huge, crooked black creatures with many legs and glittering eyes. They are all chanting and moaning, their wavering antennae pointing uniformly to the far end of the cave.

Eyes wide in fascination, the Doctor edges forward for a better view.

On the far side of the cavern, a vast stalagmite has been cut off at the base to form a great plinth or dais. On this is a stone altar. Behind the altar is a great, cup-shaped throne carved from the rock.

And in the throne sits one of the most monstrous beings the Doctor has ever seen.

Go to 85.

107

The Doctor pulls Eva's body into the molecular conversion field and activates the machine.

'What's happening to me?' she wails.

'This machine is deactivating the nanomachines in your bloodstream,' explains the Doctor. 'And quite successfully, I might add.'

Eva's muscles and skin seem to be growing back.

'The nanites have been thrown into reverse,' the Doctor says happily. 'They're repairing the damage! Oh, that's sweet. I *am* a genius!'

'Modest too,' Eva observes drily.

'And impatient. Get up and walk. You're cured. They don't call me the Doctor for nothing!'

A loud alarm suddenly starts buzzing.

'What's the matter?' Eva asks.

'The nanites are fighting back.' The Doctor checks the

read-outs. 'They're reconfiguring.'

'They're coming back?'

'Not in a way that will directly affect you, unless –'

The Doctor stares in horror as a dark cloud emerges from the machine and hovers in the air.

'What is it?' asks Eva.

'Nanite cloud,' the Doctor replies. 'Hostile, probably.'

'We have to get out of here!'

The quickest route – to the TARDIS – is blocked by the nanites. The Doctor turns and runs for the door. 'Come on – we have to get out of this place altogether.'

Eva hurries after him as the cloud hums like a swarm of angry wasps. 'I know a way off the station completely. We have a shuttle standing by on one of the launch pads. We're ten minutes away.'

The Doctor follows Eva along a short access corridor. Red

lights are flashing along the walls as the environment system detects and identifies the nanite cloud. An alarm klaxon blares loudly.

'What have I done?' the Doctor groans. 'I've created a monster! A mist monster! No, wait. I'm not going to call it that!'

'Not your fault. It was me or the nanite cloud. This way we still have a chance.'

'It'll take too long to reach the shuttle,' argues the Doctor. 'We should get to somewhere we can seal off – like the basement.'

'OK, let's go!'

Go to 46.

108

'*What do you mean, just another malignocite?*' demands the creature.

'You are the result of a scientific experiment gone wrong,' explains Professor Hardacre.

'That's putting it mildly,' says the Doctor.

'We constructed a biogenetic nanite that got out of control,' the professor continues. 'It created a billion more nanomachines, all linked together by a telepathic mind. I can put the experiment right.'

'And I can take you to a safe place,' the Doctor insists. Gambling that the malignocite will follow, he turns to leave.

The creature slithers off its throne and follows the Doctor.

The professor, meanwhile, makes his way to the nanite control hub, where he sets about deactivating the nanomachines – and every other living malignocite.

The Doctor leads the creature to the TARDIS.

'*You will free me in that?*' it says in a voice full of derision.

'It's not as innocent as it looks,' the Doctor replies.

But the creature, clearly suspicious now, tries to rip the truth straight from the Doctor's mind. The Doctor quickly pushes the TARDIS doors open and staggers inside, the malignocite following.

As he reaches the control console, the Doctor feels the creature's telepathic grip weakening. With grim triumph, the Doctor pulls the dematerialisation lever.

Go to 56.

'So many are dead,' says Professor Hardacre sadly. 'Including most of the research staff.'

'Your experiments must have gone very wrong indeed,' remarks the Doctor.

'Things could not have gone more wrong, Doctor. The nanites we created achieved artificial intelligence within three minutes of primary activation. They took over the scientific elite, devouring some for materials and energy, while converting the rest from the inside out into giant versions of themselves: malignocites.'

'I can just imagine,' the Doctor says darkly.

'They're telepathic too. They can control people using telekinesis. There's no way to beat them!'

'There's always a way.' The Doctor paces up and down the storeroom, thinking quickly. 'Is there a leader? A prime malignocite?'

'Yes. Quite a character by all accounts. For an overgrown piece of microtechnology.'

'There is a biological element, though?'

'Absolutely: genetic material from mineral deposits located deep beneath the surface of this moon.'

'Can you shut down the malignocites still under computer control?'

Hardacre strokes his chin thoughtfully. 'Well, it's possible – theoretically. But the real problem is the leader.'

'And where do I find the leader?'

'On the main lab level. I'll take you there, if you think it will help. But I should warn you: no one who has gone into that room has come out alive.'

At the Doctor's insistence, Hardacre takes him back to the main laboratory complex. They can hear malignocites moving around the base, growling and attacking survivors.

'We need to move quickly,' the Doctor says quietly. 'Are you sure you can shut down the nanites remotely?'

'If I can get to the main computer-program control centre, yes.'

'And where's that?'

'Where the malignocite leader is.' The professor shrugs. 'It's not stupid, you know.'

'We'll find out about that soon enough. I'm more worried about how dangerous it is.'

They dodge the roaming malignocites until they reach the control centre. The Doctor hesitates for a moment outside, then opens the door with his sonic screwdriver.

On a raised platform at the far end of the room is a giant malignocite, bristling with legs and eyes.

'Nice throne,' comments the Doctor. 'But, at the end of the day, you're just another malignocite.'

Go to 108.

110

Kate sags, her knees buckling under the strain. Her lips are drawn back in a rictus of pain as the creature settles into position on her neck. After a moment's weakness, however, she stands up straight again – the creature's legs flexing round her neck and shoulder as it adjusts its delicate grip.

As the Doctor watches, the alien parasite fades from sight; it's invisible.

'Kate!' he speaks sharply, his voice rich with authority. His eyes blaze intensely. 'Don't let that creature get a grip on your mind! Think of something else. Anything else! Times tables, favourite songs, TV programmes you hate. Think of *them*.'

But Kate simply raises her pistol and points it at the Doctor.

'Oh not *again*,' he says.

Kate's eyes are blank. The creature on her back has taken full control of her mind, fastening its telekinetic grip more tightly with every single second that passes. With one deft motion of her thumb, Kate switches off the safety catch on the automatic.

The Doctor stares at her. 'Kate Stewart!' he barks angrily. 'Put that gun down *now*. What would your father say?'

For a second she wavers. The gun dips. The Doctor watches her carefully, aware that he is a finger-squeeze away from a terrible injury, possibly even death. A bullet is a bullet, even for a Time Lord.

And then Kate turns and runs.

She is young and fit, and the creature controlling her is using every bit of her energy to escape. At this rate the creature will kill and discard Kate in very short order.

The Doctor, by contrast, is still weak from the mind control he has suffered.

He has a decision to make. If he chases Kate on foot, he might not catch up before the creature kills her, depending on how fast it drives her. If he doubles back and uses the

TARDIS, he will have to waste vital seconds locating her.

If you think the Doctor should run after Kate, go to 80.

If you think he'd be better off using the TARDIS, go to 101.

111

'Take a look through these,' suggests the Doctor, offering his sonic sunglasses to Jiao.

The Doctor takes a moment to study her. She's young – probably. The Doctor finds it hard to tell human ages these days. He places her somewhere between elderly and an infant and makes a concerted effort to remember her name. He knows that sort of thing goes down well with humans of all ages. Her hair is blonde and her eyes are a vibrant blue and full of intelligent curiosity. They disappear behind the sunglasses as she puts them on.

'I can see the malignocites,' she says, impressed. 'What kind of super-specs are these?'

'Sonic,' the Doctor replies. 'Among other things. They have a molecular-magnification matrix built into the lenses.'

'Wearable tech? Cool.' Jiao hands the glasses back.

'Very useful for seeing what the naked eye cannot.' The

Doctor examines the dead body carefully from every angle. 'Tell me about the malignocites.'

'We were experimenting on a new kind of pest control for crops, to help the famine worlds – at least that's what most of us were told – I had my suspicions though. One or two things just didn't add up, you know? Anyway, things got out of hand. The malignocites were only supposed to eat a very particular kind of grain parasite –'

'But somehow they self-mutated and developed a taste for human DNA?' The Doctor tuts as he moves the corpse slightly. 'It's an old story.'

'If you say so.'

'I do. I've seen this sort of thing before – nanomachinery can be very difficult to control once the numbers build up.'

'They were all connected to a base-level AI matrix. Somehow they turned into a combined intelligence.'

'A combined intelligence which is also very, very hungry,' the Doctor remarks sourly. 'How many people have been affected?'

'I think I'm one of the last survivors.'

He looks up at her. 'What was your name again?'

'Jiao.'

The Doctor clicks his fingers. 'Yes, that's it. Correct. Well done on remembering your name. But the thing is . . . Jiao, these nanites are small enough to become airborne. Like pollen. The next person they target could be you.'

Go to 103.

112

The Doctor slips into a nearby storage locker, quickly easing the door shut as the other door opens.

Someone – or something – enters the basement storeroom.

The Doctor, trapped in the confined darkness, holds his breath and listens carefully.

He can hear movement. Footsteps. The sound of someone or something with two legs, wearing boots probably, moving around the room. They move slowly, with caution, as if they're not sure what to expect in here – or as if they think someone might be hiding.

The Doctor keeps very still. The cupboard he's in is full of brushes and mops, and plastic bottles containing cleaning solution. The Doctor hopes whoever is out there is not the cleaner.

He strains to listen. He can hear the sound of doors and containers opening. Presumably the person is looking in various cupboards and lockers. How long will it be before they reach his?

The Doctor eases open the cupboard door just a crack, just wide enough for him to see out. He can see the opposite wall but little else.

Then a shadow passes into view – a shadow holding a gun.

If you think the Doctor should stay hidden, go to 89.

If you think he should jump out and disarm the intruder, go to 87.

113

A loud scraping comes from the antigravity shaft, and something dark and insect-like clambers up through the hatch.

'Look out!' The Doctor whirls, activating the flamethrower. A jet of scorching heat blasts the malignocite back into the shaft. Squealing and trailing fire, it tumbles from view.

'How did it get up the shaft?' wonders Penny.

'I've no idea –'

The smouldering malignocite crawls out of the hatch with an angry snarl.

'But it's just done it again –'

Two more malignocites emerge through the smoke, hissing and spitting.

'And it's brought reinforcements.'

'Shoot them!' screams Penny.

'No point – the first one's barely singed,' says the Doctor, backing away from the oncoming horde. He turns, aims the flamethrower at the edge of the transparent dome, then squeezes the trigger.

Flames blaze across the plasteel, which bubbles and sags quickly under the onslaught.

'What are you doing?'

'Escaping,' the Doctor says, as a hole rapidly expands in the melting window.

The malignocites hurry across the viewing platform, snapping hungrily at their heels.

'Jump for it!' cries the Doctor, grabbing Penny by the hand. Together, they leap through the hole in the viewing dome.

Go to 73.

114

The Doctor crawls painfully away from the altar, but the Malignocite Prime catches him in a telepathic grip with an impatient snarl.

'Wait!' cries a voice. 'You're making a terrible mistake!'

The Doctor looks up to see a ragged old man being dragged to the altar by a pair of malignocite guards.

'Who are you?' the Doctor asks, amazed.

'My name is Professor Hardacre. How do you do?'

'Very well, thank you. Although, to be perfectly honest, I have been better. I'm the Doctor. Tell me, professor, what are you doing here?'

'*Explain yourself, food!*' the Malignocite Prime adds.

'These two chaps brought me here,' says the professor. 'And I just happened to see what you were doing with the Doctor here. You really have to stop this madness, you know.'

'He's right,' the Doctor gasps. 'I can help you. I have a

TARDIS – a ship that travels in time and space. I can take you away from all this.'

The Malignocite Prime seethes, limbs clattering in agitation.

'Seriously,' the Doctor says, 'is this what you want? Skulking around in a damp cave eating the occasional human?'

'You need to get out more,' adds Professor Hardacre.

'*Where is this TARDIS?*'

'I'll take you to it,' the Doctor promises. 'But you have to drop all this "Malignocite Prime" stuff. It's embarrassing. You're just another malignocite – slightly more developed, but essentially still just a failed experiment.'

Go to 108.

115

'There must be another way to deal with this, professor,' the Doctor urges. 'You've broken your legs, not your brain.'

The professor coughs painfully. 'I must say, you don't beat around the bush, Doctor.'

'There's no time. This entire moon is being overrun by the malignocites. We have to find a way to stop them. And to do that we have to escape!'

'I'll never leave this cave, Doctor. Too many broken bones, and too many years lived. I haven't got long left – we both know it.'

The Doctor smiles sadly. 'Now who's not beating around the bush?'

'There may be a way for you to escape, though, Doctor. Not far from here is an antigravity lift shaft that leads directly to the gravity compensators. I've been thinking about it for some time, but there's no way I can do it myself: destroy the gravity compensators and you destroy the base.'

'Leave it to me,' the Doctor says. He bids a grim farewell to the old man, knowing that there is no other way, and climbs swiftly out of the pit. Checking that the passageway is clear, the Doctor heads towards the antigravity shaft.

When he hears a malignocite's angry growl he breaks into a run.

Go to 37.

116

'Hurry!' screams Jiao.

The Doctor opens the shuttle hatch with his sonic and they pile inside. The nanite cloud buzzes angrily behind them.

'If we blast off right away, it might not have time to get through the airlock.'

They scramble through the shuttle to the cockpit, where a group of confused and anxious scientists are gathered.

'Thank goodness you're safe,' exclaims a woman who appears to be the lead scientist, hugging Jiao. 'I'm Garon,' she says, turning to the Doctor.

'The Doctor,' he replies curtly, waving aside politeness for the sake of urgency. 'We have to take off immediately.'

Garon signals to the pilot and the shuttle slowly lifts off from the launch pad.

Jiao and the Doctor are still strapping themselves into their seats when a cry of alarm sounds from the rear of the shuttle.

On a screen showing the passenger bay, a dozen survivors are visible, seated in rows, and a sinister dark cloud is forming behind them.

'The nanites!' yells Jiao.

'They've broken through,' the Doctor says, watching in horror as one man succumbs to their blistering attack. Within seconds the man's skin and flesh has been stripped from his bones.

Garon's face is grim but determined. 'There's nothing we can do for them,' she says. 'We must seal the cockpit if we're to save those who are here.'

'No.' The Doctor has jumped out of his seat. 'Land the shuttle!'

If you think they should land the shuttle, go to 124.

If you think they should seal the cockpit, go to 33.

117

The Doctor moves forward until he's close enough to touch the squirming pupae that surround the monster. Clusters of tiny black eyes peer through the translucent skin of each grub at the Doctor as he edges past. He puts a finger to his lips. 'Quiet, kiddies. Just pretend I'm not here.'

'But you are here, Doc-tor!'

The Doctor freezes in his tracks. He looks up slowly, and finds himself at eye level with the huge creature squatting on its throne.

'You're telepathic,' the Doctor realises.

'I sensed your thoughts as you came into the cave, Doc-tor. They wriggle and squirm like my offspring.'

The Doctor looks at the blindly groping pupae and shivers. Are his thoughts worth no more than those of a giant grub?

'You are wondering who — and what — I am.'

The Doctor frowns. It had crossed his mind.

'*I am the Malignocite Prime – UnderGod of the Lower Dark.*'

'Rather a fancy title for a giant insect,' remarks the Doctor.

A psychic hiss of annoyance blasts through the Doctor's mind and he sags to his knees in agony.

If you think the Doctor should try to get away, go to 114.

If you think he should stay and find out more, go to 78.

The airlock hums open and the Doctor and Penny dart inside.

They're forced to wait in the airlock before they can move any further; the air pressure and artificial gravity will take a few seconds to equalise.

'What are we going to do now?' Penny asks, getting her breath back.

The Doctor paces restlessly around the airlock. 'We have to find a way to stop that malignocite horde.'

'Can't we just get off the moon? There's a lifeboat station not far from here.'

'It might come to that – for you. I can't leave the malignocites to thrive here. They are a deadly and almost indestructible threat.'

'Indestructible?'

'They shrugged off the flamethrower. But perhaps if we can detonate the lab's solar-power stack, or create a gravity implosion . . . well, one of those should do it. But it would destroy the base as well.'

The airlock chimes as the air and gravity finally equalise. The interior door hums open and the Doctor and Penny step cautiously into the base. The distant roars of malignocites echo through the corridors.

'We'll have to be careful,' the Doctor says quietly.

'The lifeboats may be too far away,' Penny whispers. 'We won't destroy the base *and* get to the lifeboats in time. It's got to be one or the other.'

'Or both,' says the Doctor. 'You head for the lifeboats. I'll head for the gravity controls.'

'But you'll never get away!'

'I have my own transport. It won't be a problem.'

Penny looks into his eyes. 'It doesn't feel right, just leaving you.'

'It's OK. I came here alone. I'll leave alone.'

Penny bites her lip and nods. 'The gravity controls are your best bet. They're nearest.'

An angry snarl echoes along the passageway ahead of them. A group of drooling malignocites appears at the far end and the Doctor and Penny run down the next turning in the corridor.

They reach an intersection and Penny skids to a halt. 'The lifeboats are this way,' she tells the Doctor.

'Go,' he says. 'Leave the base to me.'

She squeezes his hand briefly, then runs in the direction of the launch pads.

The Doctor heads for the opposite doorway, as the malignocites close in on him . . .

Go to 37.

119

As the Doctor becomes aware of the creatures, they too become aware of him.

Eyes open in the shadows, glittering like black jewels, and stare down at him.

He stares back.

'Do you mind?' he asks. 'This happens to be *my* TARDIS. It is supposed to be inviolate. And yet here you all are, violating it.'

A soft vibration runs through the assembled monsters. They are huddled in such close proximity the shudder flows from one creature to another, like a contagion. The eyes glow with fascination as they study the Doctor. And with something else as well . . . Hunger?

The Doctor edges towards the exit. He knows that one sudden move – perhaps even an untoward noise – will cause the creatures to swarm and very likely attack. He dare not use the guitar or his sonic screwdriver.

He reaches the exit doors and quietly opens them, hoping the creatures will flee.

They don't.

His hand touches a control. It's the Time Vector Generator – the device that controls the TARDIS's interior dimensions. He could try collapsing the TARDIS – but it's incredibly risky.

If you think the Doctor should use the Time Vector Generator, go to 102.

If you think he should try something else, go to 43.

120

'I'm staying,' Anjli whispers. 'As much as I don't want to.'

'That's good,' the Doctor replies softly. 'Because what you're about to witness is incredibly rare, quite beautiful, and very sad.'

'Sad?'

The tongues squirm on the floor, lost and blind. They curl up, winding into tight balls of glistening flesh, and then start mewling.

'They're not tongues, are they?' says Anjli.

'No. They're infants.'

The creature looms over its offspring, weeping oily black tears from its bulging eyeballs. The tears drip like thick, sticky mucus on to the infants, causing them to wriggle in excitement.

'It's feeding them one last time,' the Doctor says. 'They've outgrown the mother beast. They're on their own now.'

The mother beast growls and retreats, slumping back against the basement wall. Its eyes are shrinking, like rotten fruit. The rims are dry. The mouth hangs open, empty, panting.

'Is it going to die?'

The Doctor nods sadly. 'I'm afraid so. It's the circle of life, as an old friend used to say. The parent has done its job. Now is the time of its children.'

The creature gives a last, long rattling breath and lies still. Its eyes are clouded and lifeless.

'We don't belong here,' Anjli says. 'We should never have come to this moon.'

'It's time to leave,' the Doctor agrees.

Carefully and quietly they walk out of the room, leaving the young aliens to crawl away into the shadows.

THE END

121

'*Caves,*' says the creature.

The Doctor's eyes narrow. 'You're sure?'

'*Of course I am. I know that moon well. The cave system that runs through the rock is long and complex. Away from the light, a lichen grows on the rock which can be used to cure you.*'

'I hope you're right,' says the Doctor, throwing the lever that will materialise the TARDIS.

'*You have nothing to fear,*' the creature tells him morosely. '*The poison in your system will have lost all its effectiveness. If it hasn't killed you by now, then it never will.*'

The Doctor considers this carefully. He does feel better. 'What about you?'

'*I still need what is in the caves.*'

The TARDIS lands and the Doctor steps out into near darkness. It is cold and smells damp. Typical cave.

The light of the TARDIS pours out from behind him,

casting his long, angular shadow over craggy walls.

The creature crawls out of the police box. '*This way*,' it says, moving into the shadows.

The Doctor closes the TARDIS door and follows the strange entity as best he can. Some of the caves are very low, forcing him to bend low. At times he has to crawl on all fours, tearing holes in the knees of his trousers.

'I have to say, this isn't very dignified. I'm over two thousand years old, give or take a few billion.'

There is no answer.

'Hello?' the Doctor calls out. The word echoes back at him as he stands up. The creature has disappeared!

Go to 34.

122

He doesn't fancy getting trapped in a lift. There are only ever two ways out – up or down – and in the Doctor's long experience two ways out are seldom enough.

He slides across the tile floor until he reaches the doorway, activating it with his sonic. As the door swishes open, he topples through, finding himself at the top of a narrow flight of metal steps.

He bumps down the first few on his backside, yelping on each step. Then he's twisting, tumbling, bouncing down the rest of the steps in a tangle of long arms and legs.

No time to worry about that though.

At the bottom he climbs slowly to his feet and looks around. He's on a concrete landing. There are more steps leading down. The Doctor takes these stairs more carefully, wincing with each painful step. It gets darker and colder the lower he goes. He hears strange noises around him, but he can't tell if they're just the echoes of his own descent.

Eventually, he reaches the ground and, to his great dismay and consternation, finds himself at the entrance to a cave.

Go to 34.

123

The Doctor stares down the barrel of Kate's automatic. 'Can't we talk about this like civilised people? I thought you were one of the better humans.'

Kate's eyes narrow. 'You don't do yourself any favours, Doctor.'

'It has been said. Daleks, Sontarans, Ice Warriors . . . they're all so easily offended.'

'I'm beginning to sympathise.'

'At least the Cybermen are impossible to offend.' The Doctor winces slightly as a memory comes to him. '*Almost* impossible. There was that time when . . . well, let's just say they've never forgiven me for inventing the Glitter Gun.'

'You're rambling, Doctor.'

'I'm not rambling. I'm trying to distract the alien creature clamped to the back of my neck.'

'I've had enough of this,' Kate says. She lowers her pistol

and speaks into her mobile phone. 'Grey Division. Target the Doctor. Any sudden moves he makes that aren't directly authorised by me, shoot to kill.'

The Doctor looks aghast. 'What? What did you just say? Shoot to kill?'

'There's twenty UNIT snipers looking at you through crosshairs right now, Doctor. It's time to give up.'

The Doctor looks down at his chest. There is a cluster of red dots on one side – and another cluster on the other.

'Laser targeting,' Kate explains. 'With enough high-velocity projectiles aimed at both hearts to take out a Time Lord. Several times, if necessary.'

'Your father would never have done this,' the Doctor mutters sourly.

'Maybe you never gave him reason.'

The Doctor gazes around the area. Now he can see them:

darkly clad soldiers in helmets and goggles. Assault rifles trained on him.

'I'm disappointed in you, Kate,' he says.

'The feeling is mutual. You've brought a malevolent alien mind parasite to my planet, Doctor.' She licks dry lips. 'It's my duty to defend it, you know that.'

The Doctor frowns. The creature can sense the danger. It's preparing to kill him – or attack the humans. Or probably both.

'Hands on your head, Doctor. Get down on your knees.'

Go to 94.

124

'Land the shuttle!' the Doctor says. 'We're trapped up here – we need to get on the ground.'

The pilot starts to bring the shuttle round in a steep, banking turn, heading for the launch pad. More screams can be heard coming from the passenger cabin. On the screen, a woman is enveloped by the nanite cloud and, in a storm of black vapour, reduced to a skeleton.

'It'll kill us all,' says Jiao. 'Hurry!'

The pilot wrestles with the controls and the shuttle banks again.

'Don't bother with going back to the launch pad,' says the Doctor. His eyes are fixed on the door connecting the cockpit to the cabin, waiting for any sign of the nanite cloud. 'There isn't time. Put us down anywhere you can.'

The pilot brings the shuttle down in a steep dive – too steep. 'Brace positions!' he shouts. 'We're coming in hard!'

'Doctor!' cries Jiao. 'The nanite cloud – it's coming through!'

Wisps of oily black smoke are curling out from beneath the door seal.

The Doctor grabs the flight controls and helps the pilot to steer the shuttle towards the moon's craggy surface. The ship screams to a crash landing, sending everyone sprawling as it breaks apart.

Go to 41.

125

The Doctor emerges into a glowing cave.

The exposed rock is covered with some kind of strange, fungal growth that appears to contain a glowing chemical. The light is sickly and green.

'I'm feeling a bit sickly and green myself,' the Doctor confesses. But so, it seems, does the creature on his back: the telekinetic grip feels looser, the mental presence lessened.

'What is it?' wonders the Doctor. 'Is it the fungus?' He touches the glowing growth with his fingers, smells it, listens to it. 'What is it about this stuff that bothers you?'

The creature is struggling. It peels off the Doctor's back with a painful gasp and slithers to the floor.

'The TARDIS knew it!' realises the Doctor. 'It's brought us to these caves because it knew you couldn't stand the fungus!'

The Doctor scoops a handful of fungus from the nearest rock wall, and holds it out to the creature.

It hisses and recoils like a snake from a flame.

'Ha! Go on, be off with you!'

The creature snarls and crawls away into the darkness, leaving the Doctor alone.

'Huh,' he mutters. 'Call yourself a monster? Come to think of it, what *do* you call yourself?'

Forever a slave to his own curiosity, the Doctor wanders after the creature.

Go to 34.

'You poor creatures,' says the Doctor as he walks along the rows of cages. 'Who would experiment on living things like this?'

The rats scurry around the cages – those that still can. Some are so mutated that they can barely move. The Doctor's frown has never been deeper or darker. He wonders if there is anything he can do for these wretched animals and then stops suddenly, alerted by a strange noise.

It's coming from the other side of the room.

There is an airlock door there, with a large glass panel obscured by a thin mist of condensation.

As the Doctor approaches the airlock, something moves behind the cloudy glass.

Taking a large spotted handkerchief from the pocket of his jacket, the Doctor carefully wipes away some of the condensation and peers through the glass.

He is met by something dark and hideous staring out at him from the other side.

With sudden force, the creature smashes through the airlock glass and towers over the Doctor.

Go to 35.

127

The Doctor comes to a sudden stop, causing Eva to crash into him.

'Wait,' he says, 'what's this?'

He's pointing to an elaborate airlock system set into the junction of the wall and ceiling. A ladder leads up to a hatch marked EMERGENCY ONLY.

'Lifeboat,' Eva tells him simply.

'You have lifeboats on a moonbase?'

'In case of emergency evacuation. If the personnel need to get away in a hurry – due to a hull breach or a generator meltdown, say – there are these pods located in all main access corridors.'

'Programmed to launch into space and enter a safe orbit until help comes, no doubt,' nods the Doctor. 'Perfect. Up you go.'

Hearing a roar from the malignocite creature, Eva starts up

the ladder immediately. 'You mean we're just going to wait around in orbit for some kind of rescue?'

'You are,' the Doctor tells her, urging her further up the ladder. 'I'm staying.'

'Staying? Why?'

'I need to sort this out down here. You'll be safer up there. Now hurry up – the creature's coming!'

The malignocite appears at the end of the corridor and roars when it sees them.

Eva hurries through the airlock into the lifeboat. The hatch slams shut and pressurises, and the Doctor hits the emergency release control. There's a metallic bang and a whoosh of air, and the lifeboat is launched into space. Eva is safe.

But the malignocite has almost reached the Doctor, its long, multijointed legs reaching out for him.

Go to 48.

128

'If you want something doing,' grumbled the Doctor ruefully, 'do it yourself.'

There was no alternative. In the absence of a suitable antidote, he would have to cure himself. It wasn't impossible for a Time Lord. In certain, self-induced curative trances, Time Lords could use their regenerative powers to purge their own bodies of deadly toxins. But it was risky. Too deep a trance and the Time Lord might never wake up. Or they could accidentally start a full bodily regeneration.

'That would be awkward,' mutters the Doctor, closing his eyes.

He takes a series of deep breaths and enters a trance-like state, eyes wide open but showing only the whites.

The Doctor's subconscious mind searches through every cell of his body, seeking the impure or the tainted, and triggers a tiny, individual regenerative process in each. Eventually every alien toxin is eliminated from his body.

After a while the Doctor's eyes snap open and he takes a gulp of air.

'That feels better,' he says. His voice echoes eerily. He gives the air a sniff. 'And I think I can smell fresh air.'

His nose leads him to a low hatchway. Opening it, he peers inside and finds a narrow air duct. This will take him straight back up into the laboratory complex.

It's a tight squeeze but the Doctor manages to get into the ducting and starts to climb.

Go to 24.

OUT NOW

BBC
DOCTOR WHO
CHOOSE THE FUTURE

NIGHT OF
THE KRAKEN

JONATHAN GREEN

Your story starts here . . .

Do you **love books** and **discovering new stories**?
Then **www.puffin.co.uk**
is the place for you . . .

• Thrilling adventures, fantastic fiction
and laugh-out-loud fun

• Brilliant videos featuring your favourite authors
and characters

• Exciting competitions, news, activities,
the Puffin blog and SO MUCH more . . .

www.puffin.co.uk

 **Listen**

Do you love listening to stories?

Want to know what happens behind the scenes in a recording studio?

Hear funny sound effects, exclusive
author interviews and the best books
read by famous authors and actors
on the **Puffin Podcast** at
www.puffin.co.uk

#ListenWithPuffin